LEVELING THE FIELD

KTS #3

ELISE FABER

LEVELING THE FIELD
BY ELISE FABER
Newsletter sign-up

KTS SERIES

Prequel Novella
Fire and Ice (Hurt Anthology)

Full Length Books
Riding The Edge
Crossing The Line
Leveling The Field
Scorching The Earth (December 28th, 2021)

CHAPTER ONE

Jesse

BLEARY EYES WERE the least exciting side effect of being a secret agent.

Gunshot wounds sucked, but at least they made someone seem tough. Burning, aching eyes that came from staring at a computer screen for hours on end sounded far less intimidating.

Then again, despite my size, hardly anyone found *me* intimidating.

I was a giant Raggedy Ann doll—red hair, pink cheeks, freckles. Unfortunately, I was also six feet tall and, as one lovely ex-boyfriend had said, "built like a brick shithouse."

Such romantic sentiments.

Probably why I was still single.

Of course, even aside from the Raggedy Ann and brick shithouse vibes, being a secret agent didn't exactly mean my love life was rocking.

Kind of hard to get close to people when I had to hide half of my life.

Okay, so, if I were being truthful, my job was much more than half my life. It was . . . the entirety of my existence.

Sighing, I rubbed my eyes, closed down my computer, and stretched.

My entire team and I had been working even longer hours than normal because . . . we had a traitor in our midst. *Two* traitors, actually. One who we'd known about, and one—

"Fuck," I whispered, shoving away from my desk and swirling my chair, staring out the dark window.

Because the other traitor had been my friend, my teammate.

So now the question was, how far and deep did the rot go?

Did I need to look over my shoulder with people I'd once never hesitated to trust with my back? How could we move forward when we kept having to look behind us to make sure that a knife wasn't going to find its way into our spines?

How did I work here, *live* here without being in a constant state of alert?

My sanctuary.

The one place where I'd never felt judged for being me.

And that sanctuary was gone now.

But we'd get it back. I was determined that we would excise the traitors, and my teammate, Lily, and I had been working on ferreting out any remaining collaborators at KTS.

We'd investigated every angle, we'd thought about every possibility.

But even then, I still couldn't be sure that I had considered them all.

There must be something I was missing, something that I could plan for, something . . . I wasn't going to find tonight because I was too freaking tired.

There was a knock at the door, and I spun my chair back to face the door, which was just sliding open to reveal a gorgeous, green-eyed man, his grin absolutely contagious. I found myself grinning back . . . along with stifling the urge to run my fingers through the stubble lining his jaw.

"Leo." I waved him in, despite my fatigue. "When did you get into town?"

"Just tonight."

"That's awesome." My smile didn't fade. "It's really good to see you."

Leo, who'd been a member of my former team before I'd shifted gears and landed under the direction of my current commanding officer, Hannah, smiled back. "It's good to see you, too, Jess."

I nodded.

Waited.

He just stared at me.

Which was a problem. Because the man had the dreamiest green eyes I had ever seen. They were pools of blazing emerald, a shocking contrast to the deep olive of his skin. And his smile —that one he'd just unleashed on me—well, I wasn't a woman who swooned over a man, but *this* one? He'd always made me hyperaware of his presence, desperate to be more than friends with him.

But he'd been a teammate.

And further that, I was *me*.

I wasn't cute. I wasn't curvy. I was . . . strong.

I had broad shoulders and muscular thighs. I could program an explosive—or take one apart—in seconds to minutes, depending on how complicated they were, but I wasn't a woman who inspired attraction in a man.

I was the funny friend.

The great buddy to hang out and have a beer with.

Which was fine. I loved myself, loved the strength I'd worked hard for. It was just . . . part of me wanted the romance, wanted the fancy dress, wanted the man who thought I was the most beautiful woman on the planet.

Well, everyone had their fantasies, and I wasn't immune,

and in the meantime (because that *was* and would most definitely *always* be a fantasy), I'd focused all of my energy on being a good agent, a good teammate, and a good friend, all in that order. But none of that gave me any clue how to proceed with this conversation.

"Um, did you need something?" I asked.

He shook his head.

I waited. Again.

He smiled. *Again.*

And heat coiled in my abdomen, my thighs clenched together. I could have sworn I smelled him from all the way across the room.

Then he crossed to me, tugged me up into his arms, and for one moment . . . *for one moment* I thought that perhaps the fantasy in my mind might be for real. That he was a heartbeat away from declaring that he had always loved me and then he was going to swipe a hand across my desk, lay me across the table, and have his merry way with me.

But . . . fantasies.

Because that *one moment* passed.

He released me, stepped back, and punched me in the shoulder. Not lightly either, but hard, like one dude would punch another. It didn't hurt . . . not physically anyway. "I'm your new teammate, Jess!"

Then he punched me again.

And I felt my heart crack . . . just a little bit.

Because it had only been a fantasy. *Just* a fantasy.

And maybe if I kept telling myself that, it wouldn't hurt so much.

CHAPTER TWO

Jesse

"So, WE BUSTED THROUGH THE DOORS," Leo said.

"Then what happened?" Hannah, my team leader, asked, leaning closer, her beautiful face displaying her rapt attention.

Lily, the last of our trio of women on our five-person team, was equally entranced.

God, he even enthralled the lesbians.

It was enough to make me want to punch him.

I made a face, because he'd probably punch me back, and the man had fists like Thor's hammer, *and* nothing like chivalry would stop him. We were agents in life-and-death situations on the regular, and we'd been trained to view anyone as a threat— gender and age aside.

If I went after him, he'd come right back after me.

And then he'd probably pin me to the ground, and I'd feel all the hard lines of his delicious body pressed to mine, and I'd be in an even worse spot than I was now.

Aching and wanting.

Instead of just . . . aching and wanting.

Fucking hell, Harrison, I thought. *Get it together.*

"Then we hit the fucking deck because some dumbass missed the trip wire, and the world exploded around us," he said, taking a sip of his beer.

"Who was the dumbass?" Lily asked.

He didn't miss a beat. "Me."

Lily and Hannah roared, and even Linc cracked a smile, though I knew he was more than distracted because his girl-friend and fellow medic, Olive, was currently out on a mission with her team.

Just reconnaissance.

But there was a risk with every mission, and Linc loved Olive more than life itself.

So, he'd worry until she got back.

What *I* wouldn't give for someone to worry about me. I'd never had that, at least not outside of my teammates' friendship and the general watching of each other's backs so we didn't die. As a foster kid, I hadn't had a real family, not being in and out of homes all the time after my mom had died.

My family, they weren't . . . good people.

And for a long time, I hadn't thought I was good either.

But I'd long ago shed that veneer. I'd gone into the military, had excelled, and then had been poached by KTS.

Then had never looked back.

Who wouldn't want to be part of the premier military force in the world, albeit a secret one? Though, I supposed, being secret was part of the appeal. To feel like part of a secret club of awesomeness, especially when I'd spent a long time feeling particularly *un*awesome.

And *that* wasn't a track I wanted to revisit, even if just being around Leo brought to light all those unawesome feelings.

I wanted to be confident and unaffected.

I wanted to be able to jump into the conversation, to ignore my feelings . . . well, at least I knew I was good at the last. I'd been ignoring my feelings for years.

"I've still got the scar," I blurted, earning three pairs of eyes turning in my direction, and yeah, they were my team, but no, I wasn't necessarily comfortable with all that staring.

Especially when one of those sets was a gorgeous green pair.

A trace of regret went across his face. "I'd forgotten about that."

I hadn't.

The piece of shrapnel had slit straight through my thigh, too damned close to my femoral artery for comfort. It had been the first time Leo had put his hands on me, and I was a sick fuck for having enjoyed it.

Just for a moment.

Before the tourniquet and the pressure and the whole nearly dying thing.

I shrugged, knowing I'd just made things weird and scrambling for anything to say that would turn the conversation back to something relaxed and normal. "Trust the explosives expert to get down and dirty with the bomb." A beat, my lips forced up into a smile. "Plus, it's a cool scar."

Silence.

Then Hannah and Lily laughed, Linc smiled again, and Leo . . . his face softened.

For me?

No. He probably had gas, or something equally unappealing, and it just made his expression do that . . . that . . . *thing*. Certainly, that was more likely than the fantasy scenario I was weaving through my head—that he was getting all soft and gooey, just for me.

So not happening.

On that pleasant thought, I reached for my bottle of beer, drained the last sip I'd been nursing, saved for just this moment (in case I needed an exit), and stood. "I'm beat," I said, inching toward the door. "See you all in the morning."

Hannah's eyes narrowed, just the slightest, going from the bottle to my face, studying me for who knew what.

Okay, *I* knew what.

She'd picked up on something, was nosy as hell, and wanted my deep dark secrets.

Good thing I was excellent at hiding them.

"Night," she said after a few heartbeats, Lily echoing her, Linc nodding, and Leo . . . *my* dumbass got ensnared in those emerald eyes, his gaze searching mine for one brief moment before I managed to pull my stare away.

"Night," I repeated.

And then I was out.

CHAPTER THREE

Leo

THE GIRLS WERE COOL.

Really cool.

I was used to being surrounded by women, though not so much in my work environment. Typically, there was one woman on a team, sometimes not *even* one. Yes, there were women sprinkled throughout KTS, but during my tenure here, every one of my teams had been all male until Jess had joined my former unit. At least until this one, where Linc and I were the minority. So yeah, the gender dynamics were changing.

And now the Georgia base had two teams where the majority were women, which was . . . cool? Yeah, that.

A little strange?

Yeah, that, too.

I'd stayed just a few minutes after Jess took off, jetlag hitting hard and knowing that I'd been brought in to fill a hole left by some big shoes. That hole was good and bad. Good because Jack, the agent I was replacing, had been generally well-liked . . . at least, until he'd proved to be a traitor, who was putting agents and KTS as a whole at risk, taking their resources away from taking down the bad guys and putting them toward tracking down the turncoats who'd begun working with *those* bad guys.

Which was also the bad.

Having to prove I wasn't one of them.

Having to track down agents I might have once considered friends.

Now I walked slowly down the hall, making my way to the rooms I'd been assigned here, and though I was tired, I knew it was going to be hard for me to settle down and actually sleep. That was normal—the itchy, prickling feeling under the surface of my skin, pushing me to go out and find a mission, to take down some of the assholes KTS had their eye on, and if not that, then to find someone to fuck, to burn off that energy until I was ready to crash.

Except, I'd been here for *one* day.

I'd spent that time learning the base, getting my shit set up and ready to go—my office with its tech, my room with my clothes in the drawers and some snacks in the small pantry.

Then Hannah had briefed me on our team's directive—to ferret out any additional traitors at KTS.

Small task, that.

One that forced us to look deeply at the people who we were supposed to trust with our lives.

Shit-show, this was.

And Yoda, now I sounded like.

Snorting, I made my way down the hall, scanned my keycard to enter the living quarters area, just in time to see Jess pushing into her rooms.

Right next door to mine.

"Jess!" I called.

She spun to face me, dark smudges beneath her eyes. "Hey, Leo."

"Did you want . . ." I trailed off, not really sure what I wanted to ask.

A weary smile curved her lips. "Let me guess. You're tired, but not tired."

I shrugged.

Her deep blue eyes twinkled with amusement, and she shut her door with a soft *click*. "Come with me."

I stepped up next to her, letting her lead me through the hallways and then out through a side door. The air was cool, and she tilted her head back, inhaling deeply. Her skin was silver in the moonlight, and I froze, mesmerized by her profile. A delicate nose. Lush lips. A slender column of a throat.

My cock twitched, and I blinked, stepped back a full pace, glaring down at the organ in question.

What the *fuck*?

Seriously, *what* in the actual fuck was that?

This was Jess. My friend. She was funny and kind and a great agent. And she was . . . asexual and totally off-limits.

Right.

She rolled her shoulders, nearly as broad as my mine, and stepped forward. Jess was strong, only a few inches shorter than me, and though her face was pretty, her body type wasn't my typical. That typical being slender and waifish, small enough to be able to toss around, pin against the wall. Not tall and muscular, who'd kick my ass if I attempted to do any such hauling.

My cock settled.

See? I thought. *Just the jetlag. Well, that and the fact that I haven't been able to fuck anyone for a while.*

Fucking biology.

Prompting errant erections and shit.

"This way," Jess said, turning to the right and leading me through the dark yard.

I could make out the shadows of the training course in the far corner, the glass-enclosed swimming pool in the distance. We moved beyond both of them, and she used her keycard to enter a door just on the other side of the yard.

She flicked on the lights.

It took a moment for my eyes to adjust, and then when I saw where she'd brought me, I could have kissed her—

No, not kissed her.

Hugged?

No. That would be awkward, too.

Um . . . give her a high-five.

Yup, definitely. Just a high-five.

I surveyed the target-shooting course then turned back to face her.

"What do you think?" she asked, nibbling at the corner of her mouth. Which circled back to the whole kissing her thing, and seriously. What the fuck? Maybe it was the Georgia air. Maybe I was just pent up.

But why had my body just decided to realize that Jess was a woman?

Why now?

I deliberately ignored my dumbass dick and put my hand up for that high-five. "I think my new teammate knows exactly what I need."

"Benefit of also being your old teammate," she said, dutifully smacking my palm before turning away and twisting her red hair into a low bun, securing it with a band that she'd had around her wrist.

Pale skin dusted with golden freckles.

She had a small tattoo on her nape, almost completely hidden in her hairline, one I hadn't seen before. Before I knew it, my fingers had lifted, tracing the small line of text.

Obstinate, headstrong woman.

Jesse spun at the contact, something in the depths of those blue eyes that had me looking closer.

Then it was gone, and her brows lifted. "What?"

"New ink?"

A shrug, and she grinned, going to the rack on the wall, and pulling out some throwing knives, setting them on one of the stalls' counters. "Best out of three," she said.

I ignored the guns, the crossbows, the stars, the hand arrows, the hatchets, and the other throwing weapons to pick up an identical sheaf of knives, and took the stall next to Jess. "Best out of five," I countered.

"Always gotta one-up, huh?"

"You know men. The bigger, the better."

A roll of her eyes. "Then we'd better make it best out of seven million."

Chuckling, I pulled out a knife, weighed it on two fingers to check the balance. This would be child's play for us in the temperature-and-wind-controlled room. No Mother Nature to cope with. No bad guys running at us or firing bullets in our direction. Just skill and accuracy. "Deal," I said. "You call."

She pushed a button that sent the dummies in front of us rolling back, *way* back, increasing the challenge . . . and the size of my grin. "Left hand. Heart. Right eye. Right thigh."

"That's only four."

Her eyes came to mine. "Dick."

"Rude."

She snorted, playing her knife over her fingers, the silver of its blade flashing in the bright lights. "I *mean* the fifth target is its dick."

"Should I be grabbing mine in fear?"

The knife flew through the air, unerringly sinking into the dummy's dick—or where the dick would have been if it'd had one, and I actually had to clench my hand into a fist in order to not give in to the urge to cover my cock.

She turned her head, her mouth curving up. "Maybe." A beat. "Your turn."

I pushed all thoughts of my dick out of my brain (and seriously, but this interaction had been filled with far too much cock talk), adjusted the grip on the knife, aimed for the right eye.

And made the shot.

Jess laughed, picked up the next blade.

"What?"

"Nothing." She threw the knife, matched my shot on the right eye.

I aimed. Threw. Hit the left hand. Glanced at her.

A smirk, her fingers drifting over the blades. She barely looked as she launched the next knife . . . and it sank into her dummy's hand.

I hit the right thigh.

So did she.

I moved onto the easiest shot—the heart. The blade sank in with a solid *thunk.*

Jesse didn't miss a beat as she tagged her last target, then crossed her arms, and turned to face me as I snagged the final knife and aimed. I released the weapon, watched it spin through the air, and . . . *miss.*

Not completely.

It hit the dummy's groin, but it wasn't in the weird androgynous crotch area where the fictional dick should reside.

Jess laughed.

"What?" I asked, a blip of annoyance creeping in.

"I knew you couldn't do it." More laughter, this time filling the air. "Even in target practice, guys are too attached to their dicks."

I pushed the buttons to bring the dummies back to us. "For good reason, with women like you around," I muttered, my ego just the slightest bit bruised when she did nothing but continue laughing as she retrieved her knives.

"Cheer up, Leo. I know you hate losing. We've got four more rounds," she said, stacking the blades. "Well, only two, really, since I'm going to win the next two. But anyway"—a smirk—"it's your turn to call."

I named the targets—not the dummies' dicks, and for the record, *not* because I was too attached to my own, but because it was too big of an area to aim for.

This needed to get harder.

Jess's face filled with approval. "Making it tough?"

I hefted the blade, eyes focusing on the bottom lip. That was the hardest, so I'd get that out of the way first.

I threw. Hit.

She threw. Hit.

And as the hours rolled by, we kept at it.

CHAPTER FOUR

Jesse

MY EYES WERE BLEARY, and my hands were aching, but I took a deep breath and aimed at my dummy.

Poor guy was looking a bit worse for wear.

He was designed to take a beating, but Leo and I had gone far past the five rounds (which, by the way, *I* won, hands down), and just kept on throwing, trying to one-up each other because we were both secret agents and we had egos.

Good times.

I threw, and the knife sailed through the air, sinking into the tiny spot on the right cheek that he'd called out.

Then I yawned.

Leo glanced at me, stuck his final knife into the sheath. "We should call it a night."

"I'm"—another yawn—"fine."

He brought the dummies in, made short work of stowing his blades, then nudged me out of the way to take care of mine. A moment later, he was stowing them back on the rack.

"Come on," he said, glancing at his watch. "It's nearly one, and I don't think you've gotten much sleep since it all went down."

It being everything with Daniel and Jack and the shitshow we were now involved in. "I'm—"

"Fine," he said. "I know. You're always fine."

I winced.

"What?" he asked.

For some reason, him thinking I was always fine sliced deep. Inside, I felt very *not* fine, what with Daniel and Jack and traitors, and with Leo here, unnerving me, making me feel inadequate and ridiculous for crushing on a man who was so far out of my realm that it wasn't even funny. Him thinking I was good meant that he didn't see through the mask I put up, didn't see who I was beneath. Which was . . .

I stifled a sigh.

Typical, because I'd spent a long ass-time cultivating that shield. The one that showed the rest of the world I was completely and utterly unaffected. Growing up, it hadn't been in my best interest to show weakness. So I'd become strong, unaltered by the events around me. I think it was one of my strongest characteristics, and most definitely, one that made me a good agent.

Things went to shit?

I held it together.

A bomb counting down, readying itself to explode, seconds ticking by . . . and I could be counted on to cut the right wire.

So, it wasn't a surprise that he took me at my word.

Because I *had* just been about to say I was fine. Again.

But that stupid little girl inside me, the one who used to hide in the library and read fairy tales and fantasy novels, who embraced the happily ever after and wished to be special and extraordinary, wanted him to see through my barriers.

Stupid, huh?

Not that I could tell him that. Not that I could tell *anyone* that.

What I could continue doing?

Being fine.

"It's just my wrist," I said with a shrug. "The old break aches sometimes."

That, at least, wasn't a lie. Even though I'd hurt it in the lamest sort of way and seriously despised bringing it up.

How, one might ask?

And if I happened to admit it (something I only did when seriously pushed or was severely drunk), I'd done it falling up a staircase.

Twice.

So much fun.

I was supposed to be a mythical secret agent, and I couldn't even ascend a staircase properly. Go me. I'd broken both bones in my wrist because I tried to catch myself and instead had missed the railing and fucking Gumbied my way into stomping on my own arm.

So much shit.

As in, I'd been given so much shit for that klutz adventure.

The only good thing I'd gotten out of it was two days on the beach when the team had needed to surveil a hotel, and I'd been given lounge chair duty.

Spending that time overlooking the Mediterranean hadn't been the worst detail I'd ever had.

The cast had been itchy and sweaty, though.

I started to the door, but warm fingers wrapped around my wrist.

"That still bothers you?" he asked, and I was gaping at the feel of those calloused fingers on my skin, unable to form words, so instead I just nodded.

He lifted my arms, frowned down at the formerly broken arm. "You have tiny wrists."

My brows drew together, and that loosened my tongue. "Um, okay, weirdo."

Leo chuckled, ran his thumb over the bump there, the one

that never went away, even after the six weeks in the cast. "I still can't believe that you managed to do that to yourself." He fought a smile . . . and lost.

Self-preservation had me tugging my arm free. "And how lucky for me that it was caught on surveillance."

Another chuckle, warm and rough and sliding down my spine.

"Come on," I said, putting a little more distance between us as I made my way to the door and opened it, indicating for him to go first as I flicked off the lights and closed up behind us.

The moon was out, and a chill had entered the air, but it felt good drifting across my skin, so much so that I tilted my head down so I could feel the breeze on my nape.

When I looked up, rolling my shoulders, I saw that Leo was staring at me.

"What?" I asked, unconsciously smoothing back my hair. My ponytail tended to get out of control with very little effort, the fine strands slipping out of the holders. Which was why I usually braided it if we knew we were going into combat. Tight and secure and off my forehead so it couldn't itch me into insanity.

He opened his mouth, something flashing and gone so fast in his eyes that I couldn't decipher it. But then he shook his head. "Nothing."

I studied him closer, but after a moment, not reading anything, I just started walking back to the main area of the base, back to our rooms. "You think you'll be able to sleep?" I asked as we moved past the training course, the pool, through the open green space that I liked to hang out in when it wasn't ridiculously humid. My favorite was a shaded corner on the far end of this space that held a cozy chair, was out of sight, and was my absolute favorite place to read.

I saw him shrug out of the corner of my eye. "I'll deal with it if I can't."

"Knock on my door if you can't," I said. "I can talk to you

about the different timer varieties on the bombs I've encountered recently. I'm sure that would put you right out."

He laughed, and we continued walking.

Then I heard it. Froze.

"Wait," I whispered, snagging his arm.

Leo went to sudden and rigid awareness, and I swore that I could feel his senses brushing against mine, searching for whatever had put me on alert.

"Not a threat," I whispered. "I'm sorry." I pointed toward the roofline, toward the direction I'd heard the screech. "There," I said, still keeping my voice down. "You see?"

He shifted closer, his shoulder brushing mine before he angled his body and moved even nearer, his head next to mine, half his chest pressed to half of my back.

My breath caught, but I pushed down the thread of heat.

Not for me.

Not for me.

"See?" I whispered again.

"An owl?" he asked, and the tone of his voice told me he was not nearly as impressed as I was.

"It's a barn owl," I said quietly. "Look at her beautiful face, and if she flies, you'll see that her wingspan is huge at almost three and a half feet."

"Why do I feel like I've stumbled onto the Discovery Channel?" he teased.

I spun, punched him lightly in the shoulder. "Asshole."

He snagged my hand, ran that calloused thumb over the inside of my wrist again. "You knew that already."

I snorted and rolled my eyes. "She's beautiful and strong, and if you can't see that, then it's your loss." With a sniff, I yanked my arm free, tossed my ponytail over my shoulder, and kept walking, leaving my pretty barn owl to her hunting.

It took me a few moments to realize that Leo wasn't next to me.

"What?" I asked, spinning back to face him.

His gaze was on the roofline, but I had the notion that he was very far away, and when he glanced at me again, there was that strange expression in his eyes again. If he were looking at anyone but me, I would have said it was desire.

But . . . he'd never *ever* shown any indication that he was attracted to me.

Plus, I'd seen his type, seen who he went out with.

And that type was fucking light-years away from me.

Ouch.

I needed to stop thinking like this, needed to focus on the traitor in our midst and return to being proud of myself and my body and the things it could do. Nothing good could come from going down this track of self-hate, and I'd spent too long crawling my way out of it in order to just let my fantasy for the sexy as hell Leo mean that I'd lost all self-respect.

I was a good agent. I was smart and capable.

I wasn't a fucking damsel who needed to get swept up off my feet onto a white horse and whisked away.

I could do the sweeping.

I could do the riding.

And that was the best gift I'd ever given myself.

"Let's go," I said brusquely. "I'm tired."

His head cocked to the side, studying me, but to his credit, he didn't say anything about my tone (which was probably sharper than it should be). He swiped his card over the reader, stepping through and holding the door open for me to enter behind him. He turned unerringly in the direction of the living quarters, and I shouldn't have been surprised that he knew where he was. We were all taught to be aware of our surroundings, to count our turns, to always know exactly where we were at any given time.

And Leo was a good agent.

His lack of appreciation for barn owls aside.

"What's the owl's name?" he asked as we walked, unlocking

our way through the doors and entering the corridor with our rooms.

I paused, considered that. "I don't have one."

"Hmm."

"What?" I asked, my feet slowing to a halt, staring up the couple of inches that separated us, taking in the stubble lining his jaw, the crisp lines of his nose, the faded scar on his temple, until I reached his eyes.

His voice was soft, took my breath away. "Something that beautiful should have a name."

My throat was tight, words stoppered up in my throat.

I cleared it, painfully. "I'll work on it."

Still. The air went still, and I could have sworn that I felt a tendril shoot from my body to his, or his body to mine, lacing us together, connecting us in a way . . .

In a way that was a fantasy.

Except, Leo stepped closer, and his fingers brushed mine.

Not the inside of my wrist, but rather tracing along the sensitive tips, making me shiver, making my knees quiver.

"I should go," I whispered as I stared into his molten emerald eyes.

His fingers still stroked mine, but then he lifted one hand, slowly traced his thumb over the shell of my ear, tucking a strand of my hair behind it. Goose bumps prickled on my skin. Heat bloomed in my middle. He moved close, that hand sliding to my nape. "Jess, I want—"

A *click* behind us signaled a lock disengaging, and we jumped apart.

Hannah slid through the door, her eyes going from Leo's to mine, to our position in the hall, separated by barely a few inches and much closer than two people might be for a casual conversation. Her brows went up, and I knew she was getting the absolute wrong idea when her expression went knowing.

He'd just wanted to talk about the owl.

Right?

But maybe . . .

No. No maybes because Leo seemed to realize what Hannah was thinking as she slipped into the hall.

He dropped his hands, said loudly enough that the entire base should be able to hear, "Thanks for showing me the shooting range." Which sounded innocuous and completely normal, I knew. Except for the way he punched my shoulder again. *Hard.* "Thanks, buddy."

If he kept that up, I was definitely going to have to start punching him back.

I nodded, saw the expression on Hannah's face twist, something like pity skittering over her features, and since I didn't want to see that, couldn't *bear* to see that, not when I'd spent a couple of heartbeats, an eternity hoping for . . .

Enough.

I forced my tone to go cheery. "Anytime, bud," I said, punching him back—*hard*—then sidestepped around him and used my key to escape into my room.

"Night," I called as I stepped inside.

"Night," Hannah said.

Leo didn't say anything.

Which was just as well.

CHAPTER FIVE

Leo

BEAUTIFUL AND STRONG.

And if you can't see that, then it's your loss.

I inhaled as my own door shut behind me, the fatigue of travel or the day spent trying to learn the base, understand my new role with the team catching up to me. My body was exhausted.

My brain . . . was reeling.

That moment in the garden. The moonlight gilding Jess's skin. The exposed curve of her neck. The way she'd smiled in triumph when she'd beaten me in five rounds. How I'd suddenly noticed how delicate her hands were, even adorned with callouses and chucking knives at a target.

It was . . . unnerving, to say the least.

"Tired," I muttered.

That was the only explanation I had for it. My body was tired, my brain was overworked, and I was out of my element.

Weird feelings were certain to abound.

I'd wake up in the morning, and all would be back to normal.

"Exactly," I said, not giving a shit that I was speaking to myself as I strode into the bathroom and cranked on the shower. I'd certainly done much worse things than lusting after Jesse, a teammate who I liked and respected.

As a friend.

With an emphasis on *friend*.

A friend who had fingers I wanted wrapped around my cock, including the calloused tips I'd felt along my own when our hands had brushed—when *I'd* ensured they'd brushed—stroking up and down my shaft.

And great, now I was hard again.

Good times.

I cranked the temperature to cold and stepped in, bracing myself against the icy water but not turning it hotter, not until my cock softened, until that desire that should not be there disappeared.

Until I was finally able to get out of the shower, dry off, and crawl into bed.

Until I was able to go to sleep.

And if I dreamed of red hair and blue eyes and kissing my way up the slender column of a creamy throat . . . then I sure as hell wasn't going to tell anyone.

Least of all Jesse.

———

RED HAIR GLEAMING in the sun.

Pale skin that was at risk of getting burned.

But almost as those thoughts flitted through my brain, I watched Jesse plunk a wide-brimmed hat on her head. It was beige straw with blue piping that came very close to matching her eyes and was absolutely out of place on a private military base filled with KTS agents.

So were the short jean cutoffs. The frilly pink shirt.

Neither should be within a hundred yards of the shooting

range, of the mock explosive that was currently spread out in front of her—a tangle of wires and timers that made my head spin just staring at it.

My feet were quiet as I came up behind her, but my shadow wasn't invisible, and she spun around when I crouched down next to her. "What are you doing?" I asked. It was an unnecessary question because I knew what she was doing, and she probably knew that, too, based on the eye roll she shot me. But I'd dreamed of her last night, of the moonlight and knives flying and red hair drifting over my naked chest.

So, the question that prompted her to speak about wires and the structure of different types of bombs gave me a moment to study her as she spoke.

Searching for that spark.

The beauty in the strength.

But . . . nothing.

I mean, objectively, I could see that she had a nice face, a pretty face, but the spark from last night was gone.

Obviously, some combination of jet lag and adrenaline from the competition at the shooting range. The cute, smiling woman going on and on about timers and their various properties wasn't the siren turned silver in the moonlight, delicate and wistful.

This was Jesse.

Strong and capable and a bit quiet, unless I got her talking about something she was passionate about.

"I figured you'd have learned everything there was to know about bombs by now," I said, plunking down next to her and resting my elbows on my knees, having to nudge away several watches and what looked to be a diagram.

"Oh, no," she said. "People are always coming up with new ways to blow shit up." A shrug. "Which means I have to find new ways to stop that from happening."

I smiled.

That was the old Jesse.

Not moonlight owl goddess Jess, but the put her head down, great teammate Jesse.

I knew what to do with the latter.

The first freaked me out.

"What's this?" I asked, picking up the diagram.

"What I've managed to piece together about the bomb that Jack detonated," she said. "The one that took out the cars and nearly killed Olive a few months ago."

I remembered reading that report.

It had nearly taken down the concrete and rebar-reinforced parking structure and had damaged more than half of the base's vehicles. It was also the reason that KTS's tech team was currently working on adding bomb-proof to the bulletproof portion of the SUVs' amenities.

She opened the box in front of her, and I watched as she pulled out the bits of the bomb she'd managed to salvage—wires, scraps of metal, a half-melted SIM card. "It was set off by a cell phone," she said, pointing at the card, "and packed with shrapnel." An inhale. "Jack supposedly didn't want to hurt Olive when the bomb went off, but he sure as hell made one that was likely to kill."

"How'd he even know what to build?"

Despair in her eyes. "I taught him."

My mouth dropped open, but before I could ask how, she went on.

"I taught a lot of agents, actually," she whispered. "I gave a fucking seminar on bomb composition and disabling." A shake of her head. "All he had to do was put the steps in reverse."

"Come on, Jess," I said, bumping her shoulder. "You know you're not to blame for that. Daniel and Jack made their own decisions."

She began stacking her supplies back into the box, folding the diagrams. "Maybe not," she whispered, "But I certainly gave him an easy road map to act on that decision."

That wasn't a lie.

Daniel and Jack *had* used the skills given to them by KTS to wreak havoc, Daniel more successfully, given that he'd brought Jack in—along with who knew how many others that we didn't yet know about. Also more successfully, since Daniel was still on the run, still somehow evading the net we'd tossed out in order to capture him.

And that meant he could recruit more people, draw more agents into his web.

Which put everyone at risk.

We needed to find him, locate any agents who were working with him, and we needed to close ranks, regroup, and get back to saving innocents instead of purging the rot from our own ranks.

"Come on," I said, snagging her arm when she'd zipped the bag up.

Her brows drew together. "I have more work to do."

I snagged the bag. "Your brain is fried," I said, recognizing the glazed-over look in her eyes from our years together in London. "You need a break, and you can get back to it later."

She nodded. "Yeah, you're right. I have a report to look over, so I should get my workout over with then get back to it."

"No."

More frowning, confusion in her eyes. "Did you need help with something?" she asked slowly. "Is that why you came over?"

No, I didn't.

I'd just finished going over some files with Hannah and had been planning on taking a swim, my London body really not happy with the heat and humidity of the Georgian weather. I was still jet-lagged, and I hadn't exactly slept well the night before, so I figured I'd work myself into exhaustion, shove down some food, and go to bed early.

But then I'd seen Jesse on the lawn, a pale blue blanket beneath her, the red hair and white skin and straw hat, and I hadn't been able to walk by.

I'd needed to show myself that last night was a fluke.

That we were friends and teammates and nothing more.

"Leo?" she prompted when I didn't immediately answer her. "Did you need me to help you with something?"

"No," I said.

Her nose wrinkled, and it was cute.

Cute was good. That was friendship level. That was teammate level.

"Okay," she murmured, going back to gathering her things. The bag closed with a *zip* and then she slung it over her shoulder. "Well, I guess I'd better get on that workout." A pause, her eyes drifting to mine. "Um . . . did you want to come with?"

I nodded to the pool. "I was going to swim."

She grinned, tapped her hat, and the shoulder of the blouse she wore, which I realized now was less shirt and more cover-up. It had little ties running at a diagonal, a shadow of some dark material outlined beneath.

A swimsuit, I knew instinctively, even before her lips curved, and she said, "Funny. I was going to swim, too." Her smile widened, and I felt my pulse speed up. "I just like to warm up in the sunshine before because—I'm going to warn you now—the pool water is frigid. No heated depths for us."

The heat building at the base of my spine was from the afternoon sun and nothing more.

"Business and training," I said, ignoring that heat and its potential causes.

She laughed. "Exactly. Pure and simple work. No pleasure in sight."

Her cheeks were pink, the freckles standing out in sharp relief. I wanted to kiss each one of them. I wanted to kiss *her*.

What?

No.

That wasn't what I wanted. It was the jetlag and exhaustion, and I was holding the fuck onto that excuse, even if it was already getting old. So anyway, I just needed to get in the cold water, to work my body into exhaustion, and I needed to find someone to have sex with.

Jesse bent over, snagged the blanket, and began folding it, and my eyes caught on the curve of her ass.

Someone to have sex with who wasn't Jess.

Because going down that route could only lead to disaster.

CHAPTER SIX

Jesse

I DROPPED my towel on the bench next to the pool, rolled my shoulders, and then made sure my ponytail was secure.

Leo was to my right, kicking off his flip-flops and tugging off his shirt.

I'd seen that chest more than once, and I knew it could easily throw me for a loop—pecs that were more than a handful, etched muscles, a dusting of hair that drifted over golden skin and disappeared beneath the waistband of his pants—or in this case, his swim trunks.

So, instead of giving me the opportunity to stare and drool and fantasize about some man who'd never looked at me twice—

Buddy.

Buddy.

I dove into the pool and started doing laps.

The water was my happy place, even despite the cold temperature. My strokes were steady and uniform, and within a few seconds, I settled into a rhythm that barely altered when Leo jumped in behind me.

I saw his body sluice through the water out of the corner of my eye, knew he'd catch up with me quickly.

Not because I was out of shape or a bad swimmer—I was neither—but because the man was liquid lightning in the water. He'd been a Seal and had always had a natural affinity for swimming—maybe the name Seal was an accurate descriptor. Tall and strong and faster and . . . blowing by me.

That was okay.

I was happy with my steady strokes, content with my endurance.

I liked feeling my muscles work, warming against the cold, my lungs burning, my body gradually growing tired.

Leo turned at the far wall, swimming back toward me, passing by my side in a flash of olive skin and black swim trunks.

I liked . . . *this*.

Leo and I had done this many times in the past.

Swimming until our limbs were heavy with exhaustion, then chowing down on whatever food was at hand. Sometimes we'd watch a soccer game, other times we'd drink a beer and shoot the shit about nothing.

Friends.

Until my heart had gotten involved.

Until I'd needed distance to close it down.

Until . . . I'd known that Leo would never see me that way.

And now he was here again, and I was struggling with shutting down that fantasy of wanting him (again).

But . . . I was in my happy place, and I had learned to take my small victories where I could, to let go of everything else.

I was me.

He was Leo.

That was the end of the story. I may like to read romance novels with their guaranteed happy endings, but I knew enough of the real world to understand that the stories I loved were complete and utter fantasy.

Same as anything happening with Leo and me.

So, I was going to enjoy my swim, push my body to the limits as I preferred, and not get out of the pool until I felt like I could barely lift my arms. The exhaustion would stifle the fantasies, make me too tired to dream.

Then I'd focus on work, on exercise, on friendship.

Leo bumped me, slowing in the water and shooting me a grin that had my already pounding heart accelerating, my warm and lax muscles going limp, my pussy clenching, and my lungs sputtering.

It took everything inside me to continue my strokes, to keep them even, to continue making my way back and forth across the pool.

But I made one more vow as I swam.

Work, exercise, friendship, and . . . orgasms.

I needed orgasms.

Leo brushed back by me again, and I knew him well enough to understand it was a challenge, to keep moving, to try to catch up. He was a dolphin cresting in the wake of a ship, playing with me, coaxing me to push myself further—with a poke to my side, a hair-covered leg brushing alongside mine, a hand sliding down my arm.

Teasing, friendly touches.

That set my body on fire, that tempted me with the promise of those orgasms.

But those releases of pleasure wouldn't come from Leo, no matter how much I might want that.

So, back and forth I swam, over and over and *over* again.

Eventually, though, my limbs were too heavy, and I knew I'd pushed it far enough. I made my way to the ladder, climbed out with shaky arms and legs, plunking my ass on the tile next to the exit as I watched Leo continue to swim.

He never seemed to tire, just drove his arms through the water, slicing through the clear blue liquid, his legs strong and powerful.

Then he was turning toward me, body angled like that dolphin again, water sluicing off him as he made short work of the ladder. He shook himself like a dog, water spraying everywhere. I didn't mind, though, I was dripping wet myself, and not just from the water.

Between my thighs, moisture pooled, desire stoked by the game in the pool, even though I knew that Leo hadn't meant it that way.

Friends. Just . . . friends.

He plunked down next to me, his chest heaving.

Mine was steadying, and it only took a few moments for his to match mine.

He bumped my shoulder. "I missed this."

"What?" I asked.

"Swimming with you," he said. "You're the only one who can ever keep up with me."

I snorted. "And by keep up, you mean feeling like I'm going to die if I take one more lap trying to pretend I can catch you?"

A grin that had my thighs squeezing together. "Yeah," he said. "Exactly that."

My hair was dripping down my back, so I stood up and crossed to the bench to grab my towel, wrapping it around my sodden ponytail and gripping it tight as I made my way back.

I started to sit again.

Fingers on my thigh halted me.

Shocked, I nearly dropped the towel when I glanced down and saw Leo's hand on my leg, his fingers stroking the scar on my thigh. "I'm sorry for this," he murmured, slowly tracing the broad pink line. "I don't know if I ever told you that, but I'm sorry you got hurt on my watch."

My lungs weren't working.

"When you got hurt," he whispered, "I—" He shook his head, green eyes coming up to mine. "It was my fault."

"No," I whispered back. "Shit happens and—"

"On me," he said softly, gently tracing that line. "I'll make it up to you."

"Leo, that's not—"

He kissed the scar, making my breath hitch, and straightened. Then suddenly, he was towering over me, his body—hot and wet and glistening and so *damned* cut—separated from mine only by the barest millimeters.

"I'll make it up to you," he said again.

And then he disappeared into the locker room.

CHAPTER SEVEN

Leo

A SCAR.

Guilt.

Painful memories.

And Jesse never failing to grant me absolution. Even though I was the reason she had that six-inch line on her thigh.

I'd kissed that line, kissed her skin that was damp and warm . . . and far too close to other damp and warm places. I'd kissed her *thigh*. What in the fuck was I doing? This was Jess. She was my friend, and I was crossing serious lines, and she would always be too fucking nice to call me on it.

I shouldn't be kissing a woman's thigh when I didn't want her.

Not like that. Not in the way a man should want a woman when his mouth was five inches from her pussy.

She was . . . not my type.

I went for pretty things in tiny packages. A woman I could lift up and fuck against the wall. A woman who was soft and sweet and shy. A woman I had to coax and tease into a smile . . . and Jess wasn't any of those things.

Except, my brain couldn't let go of the moonlight and the narrow column of her throat that was begging to be kissed, the lines of her face that were cute when she was silent but striking when she laughed. I couldn't let go of seeing Jess sitting quietly in meetings, shy coming to the forefront when pink flooded her cheeks if all eyes went to her. I couldn't let go of the kindness she'd shown in taking me to the shooting range, even when she was tired, nor the competitiveness and humor that came out when she managed to relax.

She wasn't tiny, wouldn't be an easy lift onto that wall.

But then again, she could probably hold herself up, couldn't she?

She was sweet. She was shy. She was soft—even in the places she was hard.

"Fuck," I whispered, knowing this wasn't going to work, that I couldn't go down this path and not end up hurting her.

She might be all the things—minus tiny—that I found attractive, but she was *Jesse*. My teammate, my friend, my . . . a woman I couldn't protect because she would always be out there and at risk and—

The door to the locker room opened, and I listened to the soft slap of Jesse's feet as she made her way over to the showers.

She didn't say anything, just met my gaze for one heartbeat before closing the curtain. A moment later, the water turned on, her swimsuit hit the tile, and I'd actually taken a step in the direction of that stall before I remembered myself.

Before I *remembered*.

Turning on my heel, I left the locker room.

———

I ALMOST DIDN'T HEAR the soft knock on my door a half-hour later, as I was just coming out of my shower—icy cold, for the record—the water still plinking as it made its way down the drain.

Hitching my towel around my hips, I left the bathroom and tugged open the door.

Jess stood on the other side.

Not a surprise, some part of me having known she'd come.

"You forgot these," she said, her skin flushed from her shower, her wet hair darkened and slicked back into a ponytail, and held up my flip-flops, my T-shirt.

"Oh, yeah, I got . . ." I trailed off because I almost said something like *I nearly was overrun by the urge to join you in that shower, and I don't know why I'm having these feelings for you, but I can't have them, and I ran so I didn't try to see how easy it might be to fuck you against the tile-covered wall.* "Distracted," I finished lamely.

Also, this just in. I may have a problem with walls.

Either that, or a fetish.

"Right," she said, her eyes flicking down to my towel, and I felt my cock twitch.

"I remembered—" I cut myself off before I could tell her . . . what?

Everything. I wanted to tell her everything.

"Yeah," she whispered, as though that were a complete thought instead of the roiling in my mind. "I'll see you around, Leo," she said and turned in the direction that led out of the living quarters, back toward the rest of the base and our offices.

"Where are you going?" I blurted.

She glanced over her shoulder, the muscles flexing on her back, and I was struck by the beauty in those strong lines, beauty that wasn't brought out via the moonlight, but rather whatever light she had inside her.

"I've got some work to catch up on," she said, and there was something sad in her eyes, her voice, that I couldn't let stand.

Not with Jess.

I didn't want her to be sad. Not ever.

She was too . . .

Just *too*.

"Have dinner with me," I said. "We can catch up on everything we missed over the last few years."

"I thought we did that last night," she said, one brow arching delicately.

We had done that.

"Then with the missions," I hurried to say. "I have a lot to catch up on, and not all of it is something I can read in a report."

Her eyes, Caribbean blue, studied mine before sliding over my shoulder. Her lips, lusher than I'd ever noticed before, pressed flat. "Hannah might be better suited to giving you a briefing."

She was trying to avoid this, avoid me.

I should let her.

But something inside me wouldn't let it go.

"Hannah's busy," I lied.

Eyes back to mine, that lifted brow remained.

"Please," I found myself saying, because some part of me was telling me that I couldn't let her walk away right at this moment.

Not like this.

"I'm going to be working for a few hours," she said.

"I'll come to you in two," I told her. "If you're not done, we can eat in your office. If you are, we can go search for your barn owl."

A ghost of a smile.

"Okay?"

She relaxed. "Okay."

CHAPTER EIGHT

Jesse

I GLANCED up at the sound of the knock, more of my bleary-eyed super skills coming to full effect.

It had taken me a while to focus, the sight of Leo in just a towel burned on my retina. He was gorgeous, and it was nearly impossible to focus on conversation when he was standing there, glistening drops of water slowly dripping down his torso.

But eventually, I'd fallen into the patterns of my work.

Our team's job was to try and weed out traitors at KTS. The other team we collaborated with—made up of Linc's wife, Olive, along with Laila, Ryker, Dan, and Ava—were tasked with tracking down that first traitor, Daniel (not to be confused with Dan) and what his activities were.

Hopefully, by working from both directions we would be able to make some headway.

Right now, Lily and I were focused on tracking down items on the black market that shouldn't be there, and I'd found some. Weapons that had been specially crafted by KTS techs with certain bullets and scopes that weren't available anywhere else, not to mention, were made up of special composite that our techs had created in-house and hadn't allowed on the public market.

Not detectable by metal detectors, easy to manufacture, lightweight, stronger than steel.

It was good stuff.

But now . . . it was listed on the dark web.

And it appeared that a deal would be happening nearby in the next week. Now, I just needed to figure out where it would all go down.

Leo strode into the room, a tray in his hands. "Did I give you enough time?" he asked.

Not nearly enough time. I wanted to dive into my computer and stay inside until I managed to figure out the exact date, time, and location of the deal, but that would take hours, and I was exhausted. It would be much better if I picked this up again in the morning.

"No," he said, before I could respond. "But you've had enough."

I blinked up at him, brows drawn together.

Grinning, he plunked the tray down, right on top of my papers, making me jerk out a hand to save my cell phone from ending up as fodder.

"Do you mind?" I muttered.

"Thanks, Leo," he said, "for bringing me sustenance and not allowing my stomach to go empty. You're such a good friend."

Friend.

Did friends kiss other friends' thighs?

Probably not, if one looked at this from the traditional angle, but Leo had basically been kissing an old boo-boo. I'd realized that as I struggled to focus on my work, on trying to figure out the source and the details of the upcoming deal.

At least until I came to the conclusion that the kiss meant nothing. It was a paternal swipe of the lips, and that was all.

After I'd understood that, I'd been able to dive into work.

Because I'd rather be focused on tracing IP addresses and

trolling through bank statement after bank statement looking for irregularities, on tracking down property owners and sourcing data through a twisting, winding path. I was good at details, excellent at sifting through the bullshit and narrowing in on the small, important things. That was probably why I was good at explosives. Not getting distracted by the extraneous clutter and reducing the bomb down to its individual parts—timer, detonator, combustible material.

Remove one or more of them to render it inert.

Job done.

But in this case, my task was far from done.

Not until KTS was safe and undertaking its mission again. That mission didn't include allowing dangerous weapons and tech into the hands of bad guys, and it sure as shit didn't include *working* with those bad guys.

Leo cleared his throat, and though his mouth was curved, his eyes were serious. "You're taking this personally," he murmured.

How could I not?

KTS was what I'd built my adult existence on, a bright spot after a shitty childhood worth of darkness. I'd been happy here, had made it my family, and—I stifled a sigh—just like in real life, my family hadn't stepped up.

A deadbeat dad.

A single mom who'd passed too young.

Grandparents unwilling to take me in.

Home after home after home where the bad and mediocre outweighed the good.

Always on edge, always waiting for the other shoe to drop, until . . . here. Until my teammates had become my new family. And until Daniel and Jack had ruined that.

"I don't like it when the bad guys win," I said, instead of telling Leo any of that.

We all had our own baggage and pain. Mine came from having the bonds shatter time and again. Leo . . . well, he didn't discuss his past, and I'd respected the barrier enough to never push beyond what he was comfortable with, but I knew there was something that had cut him deep from his past, something that sometimes made shadows dance across his eyes.

"None of us do," he said, patting her hand. "Now eat, and tell me what name you've come up for your owl."

He'd brought me homemade pasta with pesto sauce, a Cesar salad, crunchy sourdough bread, and a huge slab of chocolate cake. It looked and smelled delicious, and while one of the perks of KTS was that we actually had good food, so much better than my commissary days of old, this was . . . well, I knew this option hadn't been on the menu today. That he'd managed to get Cook to make it, make my favorite, that he'd *known* my favorite . . .

All of that convincing myself that him kissing my thigh was just soothing a boo-boo disappeared.

Again, I hoped.

"I don't have a name for her yet," I said, when he just looked at me, brows up. "I haven't exactly had any spare brainpower around to think of a good one."

"Hmm." A beat. "Eat." He nudged the tray closer.

"What about you?" I asked.

"I ate before I came," he said with a smile, "considering that when I knocked on your door an hour ago, you didn't even deem it polite to look up."

I blinked. "What?"

"You were so engrossed in that"—he nodded to my laptop —"I figured you could use a little more time before I dragged you off to bed."

He could drag me anywhere, and I would go.

"You were here an hour ago?"

A nod, lips curved.

"And I didn't hear you?"

A shake of his head this time. "Nope."

Damn. I must have been really out of it. "Some secret agent,"

I said lightly, even though I was cursing myself for being so off my guard. Those kinds of instincts could get me killed.

I was supposed to be aware of my surroundings at all times, even when I was in a supposedly safe place.

"Eat," he said.

I wasn't feeling particularly hungry. Tired, yes. Worried about how we'd figure out the problems at KTS. Also, yes. Confused about Leo, hoping that him being here in my office with my favorite meal meant something, even as experience was telling me that it was nothing more than just kindness. Triple yes.

"I'm not hungry," I murmured, and jerked my head in the direction of the door. "I'm sure you're tired and want to go to bed."

"Eat," he repeated. "*Then* I'll go to bed."

"I said I'm not hungry."

"I *said*"—his voice took on a sharp edge—"to eat. You need to fuel your body."

I glanced down at my body, at the hard lines and lack of curves, the broad shoulders and heavy thighs. "I think I've fueled it enough over the years," I muttered, before I could stop myself.

His eyes flared, and I could have cut out my tongue.

It was one thing to think shitty thoughts about myself, but it was another to reveal those insecurities, to speak that inner monologue aloud.

I was supposed to love my body, and at the very least, if I didn't, I was supposed to pretend I did. I certainly wasn't supposed to tell Leo any of those uncertainties.

Fire flared in his eyes.

I smothered a wince, not wanting a lecture.

His mouth opened, closed . . . and then quiet descended, long and heavy enough that I bent my head, studying the contents of my plate.

"Hedwig?" he asked.

I blinked, head jerking up. "What?"

"For your owl."

My eyes rolled as my body relaxed, the lecture not forthcoming. "You mean I should steal the name for an owl from *Harry Potter*, who by the way, isn't a barn owl at all?"

"It's not like you have a better one."

My teeth ground together. "I could find a better one."

"Prove it." He nudged the tray closer. Any nearer, and it would be on my fucking lap. "And *eat* while you're at it."

I sighed. "What's it to you?"

His hand covered mine, sparks shooting up my arm. Sparks that only I felt, since he didn't back away, didn't react, didn't come closer. "Do I need to feed you?" he asked, brows arching, reaching for the utensils.

I picked up the fork before he could, mostly to get my hand away from his, away from the imaginary sparks that only I felt. "I think I can manage."

Leo sat back, looking smug and all too proud of himself. "What's the name of that owl from the Tootsie Pop commercials?"

Since I'd just plunked a giant bite of pesto in my mouth (fuck salad for the moment, it was carbs, all carbs), I nearly choked on the noodles and sauce. But apparently my secret agent skills also extended to internal Heimlich, because I managed to both not die of pasta-related affixation and to also not spit my food out on the plate.

"Does that owl have a name?" I asked when I could speak again.

A grin. "No clue." He tapped his chin, and I found myself taking another bite, then another. My embarrassment and twisted ego disappearing into the back of my brain as delicious sauce coated my tastebuds. "Professor Owl?" he asked. Then immediately shook his head. "Nah," he said, more to himself than to me. "That's just lame."

I snorted, kept eating as he relayed even more ridiculous names.

Fluffy and Feathers, Speedy and Screech, Mrs. McFlyFace and Moonlight.

And by the time I'd finished my salad and started on the slab of cake, he'd moved onto other topics—namely, hockey and whether or not he could convince Dan to ask his sister Brit for tickets to the next game that was close.

"I heard they're going to be good this season," he said, "and it's been years since I've seen a live game."

"There are closer teams," I said, licking icing off the fork and wondering if my stomach was too full to finish the piece. Then remembering that I was never too full to finish chocolate, especially chocolate cake. "I've been watching the Breakers play."

He lifted a brow. "Weren't they kind of a joke?"

"Rebuilding years," I quipped. "Plus, their team has really gelled this year."

"When we get some time off, we'll go," he said. "It's not far."

I smiled. "I can taste the beer already."

He laughed. "There's something about watered-down beers in an arena, isn't there?"

I polished off the cake, lifted the now-empty tray, grinning because he was right. There *was* something about the excitement of live sports. The crowd, the speed, the crack of sticks and pucks, and the sharp edges of skates digging into ice.

"Yes," I agreed, "there is." With that, I stood and rolled my shoulders, yawning as fatigue slid through me now. I went through the motions of closing down my laptop, locking my reports away. I'd return the tray, sleep, and then get back at it in the morning.

"Here," Leo murmured, snagging the platter. "I'll take it back for you."

"Serving *and* cleaning up after me?"

He sketched a bow. "I'm at your service."

Laughter bubbled through me. "You're an idiot."

"Maybe." He bumped my shoulder. "But you're friends with one."

Friends. *Friends.*

And what did that say about me?

CHAPTER NINE

Leo

JESS INSISTED on following me into the cafeteria, waiting as I stowed the dirty dishes in the appropriate bins, before walking beside me back to our rooms.

She was nearly my height; her stride easily matched mine.

And she'd gone quiet again.

Usually, I just accepted those moments as Jesse being Jesse, but for the first time I wondered what drew her under, what had caused her to withdraw back into herself.

Me?

Nothing? Just the natural course of a shy woman reaching her limits on conversation?

Fuck knew that she wasn't one to prattle on.

It was just . . . today I wondered.

The halls were quiet. This base was smaller than the one in London, fewer teams living here on a permanent basis, more of them just rotating through to other locations—San Francisco, New York, Austin, Seattle, several other smaller cities in the States, many other bigger ones across the globe. So, there was just a small contingent here outside of Atlanta, in a spot that appeared at first glance to be quiet and in the middle of nowhere, but had been the epicenter for many of KTS's problems.

Today, however, it was extra quiet.

Maybe because it was late. Maybe everyone else was working on the traitors.

Maybe it was as though the rest of the universe were sleeping, giving us space to—

I blinked, shook myself, continued walking.

Even as the silence continued to grate on me.

"What is it?" I blurted as we moved into the hallway that led to our rooms.

Frowning, she looked up at me. "What is what?"

"Why'd you go quiet?"

A sniff, her lips tipped up into a smile that wasn't a Jesse-smile, and fuck if I knew what that meant. Except to say that it was wrong, and I didn't like it, and she shouldn't be smiling like *that*.

She should be smiling with that light that came from inside her. The warmth.

Not . . . the facsimile copy she was giving me in that moment.

"I'm just tired," she said. "It's nothing."

"Bullshit."

A sharp word before I even fully grasped that I'd spoken, that I'd snagged her wrist and halted her forward movement.

Soft skin.

Delicate bones.

She tugged herself free, gave me that smile again, and I would swear that it set my spine on fire. Fury? Desire? A pissed off male-response because a woman I cared about was denying me the truth? They were all twisted together, and none of it made any sense and—

"Yes," she said lightly. "It is bullshit. I wish that I never got tired." Sarcasm swept in now, and I felt the fury spark, fueling the tangle of desire. "But alas, even KTS agents get weary every once in a while."

I wasn't one for angry affection or rage-filled sex. That didn't get me off.

But Jesse's tart tone certainly gave me a vision of wrapping my hand in her ponytail, tugging her head back, and nipping at her throat until she told me every single thought that was drifting through that big ole brain of hers.

"So, anyway," she went on, striding toward her room, pushing open the door. "I'm only human, and I'm going to bed—"

"Wait," I said, catching her arm.

She turned back at the same time I moved close, and the air between us grew taut. Her eyes had flecks of gold in them, a fact I'd never noticed before.

But then again, there were so many things about her that I'd never noticed before, weren't there?

Like how her bottom lip was a slightly darker pink than her top.

How her breasts were small but rounded, and I bet they'd be more than big enough to fill my palms. I wondered if her nipples would match that bottom lip, if they would turn even rosier with the attention of my mouth.

I wondered—

A *click*.

One I recognized from last night. Someone was coming.

I released her arm, ran my knuckles over her cheek. "Good night."

A nudge had her inside, another had the door closing, and then I was turning to my own room, moving inside my own door, nodding at Linc and Olive as they walked past, too wrapped up in each other to pay me much attention.

Which I was grateful for.

Because otherwise I might have done something truly reprehensible.

Jesse was untouchable.

Especially by the likes of me.

———

"WE'LL ENTER FROM HERE," Hannah said. "You and Jesse will be on the perimeter."

It had been two days since I'd brought Jesse dinner, and I'd spent yesterday getting caught up on all the intel my team had collected to date, along with helping Lily investigate several connections between Jack's bank account and members of several mob bosses.

And avoiding Jesse.

There was that, too.

Because I hadn't been able to corral the wayward thoughts in my mind, in my dreams.

Seriously, what the fuck was wrong with me?

It was Jesse. *Jesse!*

And I'd spent the past three nights dreaming increasingly lewd dreams about a certain red-haired beauty who would speak softly of owls and could kick my ass in knife throwing.

It made no sense.

I knew it didn't.

But . . . I couldn't act on any of it. Not with Jesse. *Never* with her.

It was just as well that we were finally going to see some action. I needed to burn off some steam, needed to forget the confusing thoughts.

I needed to shoot something.

Luckily, that opportunity seemed as though it were going to present itself shortly. Jess had gathered information about KTS-grade weapons being traded on the black market, and we were hoping that we might be able to trace them back to whoever was betraying us.

Betraying *us*.

The thought had rage filling my veins, setting my brain to what my former leader, Landon, had always jokingly called Warrior Mode.

Despite the stupid name, it was true in many ways, I supposed.

My job took a certain amount of compartmentalization, and that included those times right before a mission. I needed to shut down anything extraneous in my mind, to focus on the job at hand, at ensuring our backs were covered, that my team-mates were protected.

KTS's strengths came from its collection of five to six-person teams based around the world. Those smaller groups of agents could infiltrate easier than a large contingent swarming the space, not to mention smaller teams meant they could *be* more places, could be strategically positioned around the world where we would do the most good.

But those strengths also brought weaknesses.

Smaller, independently functioning teams were easier to fracture.

Case in point, Daniel's betrayal.

And then Jack's, and the whole reason that I had switched teams.

Because I wasn't going to allow the organization that had become so fucking important to me to be destroyed from the inside out, not when we had so much good left to do in the world.

Not when I could still make a difference.

Hannah mentioned a few characteristics of the building—the entrances and exits, vantage points we could use to keep track of what was happening inside, a few pitfalls of the surrounding area—one being an actual pit that had been dug on the far side of the space.

Maybe for a septic tank.

Maybe for something more nefarious, based on the danger in dealing with illegal weapons.

I nodded my understanding, asked my questions—the timing of the deal, whether there were any interior stairs that might give one of the fuckers an exit via the second story window or the roof and fire escape—and listened while Jesse and Linc did the same, while Hannah relayed everything she had learned from the tiny, rodent-shaped drone that our tech guys had created and which she and Lily had used for reconnaissance the night before.

Everything seemed straightforward, but that appearance made my skin prickle.

These were always the sorts of missions that went FUBAR.

When it all seemed to be going splendidly, when there weren't any hiccups, or it was supposed to be an easy pickup, drop-off, *that's* when things went to shit.

"Good?" Hannah asked a half hour later.

I nodded, along with the rest of the team.

"Good," she said again, lips twitching. "Gear up. We move out in an hour."

Jess pushed up from the table next to me, her thigh brushing mine, and even in my Warrior Mode, I was still aware of that contact far more than I should be.

She paused, stacking up some papers, and I studied her face, realized with surprise that probably made me the biggest asshole on the planet, that she was actually quite beautiful. Her throat was a slender column of creamy skin, the surface like porcelain with the exception of a narrow scar that peeked out from beneath the collar of her shirt, demanding to be kissed. Her cheekbones were high and dusted with a smattering of freckles I was suddenly quite desperate to count. Her ears were delicate, adorable and tiny and elven. Her eyes . . . had I ever actually looked inside them before?

Because they were a shocking color of blue. The bright sky on an early summer morning, dusted with whirls of clouds.

Whirls?

Adorable elven ears?

A scar that demanded to be kissed? Freckles to be counted?

I blinked, glanced away before she caught me looking, and began gathering up my belongings, wondering what in the ever-loving fuck was going on with my brain.

This wasn't Warrior Mode.

This was Gonna Get My Ass Shot Mode, and—I spun when my gaze drifted to her ass, when she bent over to retrieve a pen she'd dropped—Gonna Endanger Everyone Around Me Mode.

And Jesse already had one scar from that mode. I wasn't going to be responsible for giving her another.

That more than anything recentered me.

She couldn't be hurt because of me. Not again. Not any of my teammates. Not anyone I cared about. I had more than enough guilt on that front to last a lifetime, more than enough darkness that had dug its claws into my brain.

She straightened, pen in hand, and studied me closely, only a few inches separating our bodies. "You okay?"

She had a freckle on the right curve of her upper lip.

I wanted to kiss it.

The urge was so strong that I nearly did it, nearly bent down and flicked my tongue over the spot when she touched my wrist.

With everyone else in the conference room still there.

Fuck.

Fuck.

"Leo?"

"Don't." I jumped, skittered back so fast that I tripped over my chair, nearly eating shit as I ripped my hand from hers.

Hurt crossed her face.

Hannah cleared her throat before slipping from the room, and I didn't miss the flash of pink on Jess's cheeks, the pain slashing deeper into her expression.

Fuck.

I wanted to shove one of those throwing knives from the shooting range into my kidney, as impossible as that was. I wanted to take her into my arms and kiss her. Opening my mouth to apologize, I didn't get so much as one syllable out before she lifted her chin and asked softly, "What's wrong?"

Gently.

I closed my eyes, more guilt tearing through me.

What was *wrong?* I wanted my friend, my teammate. That couldn't happen. Not even because of the work complications that might bring, but because she was Jess and I was me, and there was no fucking way that would ever work. It would never, *ever* work. I wouldn't ever allow it to work, couldn't risk it. Not with Jess.

"Nothing's wrong," I snapped. "I just don't have time for friendship today. We've got a mission, and you shouldn't be touching me . . ." I trailed off, not knowing how to finish that thought.

She shouldn't be touching me because I wanted her, and that was . . . impossible.

Fuck, I was an asshole.

A giant, blazing asshat of an asshole.

"Right," she murmured, slowly backing up, nodded. "I understand."

More guilt, stoppering up my words in my throat. "I—" I managed to force out. "It's—"

Too late.

Her expression went cold, those lush lips pressed flat, and she nodded as though having come to some decision, said, "See you in the car." A beat, derision in her blue eyes. "Buddy."

A moment later, she was gone.

And I was an even bigger asshole because I just let her go.

CHAPTER TEN

Jesse

I CLENCHED my fingers into a tight fist, trying to ignore the bitterness crawling through me.

I repulsed him.

He'd torn himself from me like I was a pile of steaming shit, as though I hadn't taken a shower in months, as though . . . I were Jesse.

And Hannah had seen.

A sharp bolt of anger, of disgust, shot up my spine, had my fist clenching tighter.

The only small victory was the fact that Linc and Lily had already gone, that the rest of my teammates hadn't caught on to my crush, to my pathetic lusting and fantasizing after Leo.

He'd lurched away.

Lurched.

At my touch, and then like an idiot, I'd pressed him, and he'd said he didn't want *me* to touch him.

And that made me feel . . .

"Fuck," I hissed. It made me want to punch the wall, to keep punching it, to use the pain of my fist meeting the hard surface to purge this feeling of fury, of disgust, of resentment and never measuring up. But the walls on base were made of concrete and thick at that. Punching one would get my ass a broken hand and a trip to the infirmary . . . and off this mission.

I couldn't lose work. Not when I had nothing else.

Which was why I did the one thing I was good at—shoved down those feelings, focused on work.

Nothing was going to change.

I was me. Leo was a teammate. Nothing more. Even if he'd brushed his knuckles over my cheek. Even if he touched my wrist and brought me dinner.

There was no *us*.

There would *never* be an us.

So, I might as well stop kidding myself and try to save the world.

At least, that was better than focusing on my own pitiful circumstances.

I detoured to my quarters, splashed some water on my face, locked down my emotions, and tucked away the fantasy that would never be.

Work.

Friends.

The word sounded bitter, even in my own mind.

But it had always been enough, would always *be* enough. Even if it wasn't what I wanted. Which was fine, because I was used to not getting what I wanted.

And with that auspicious thought, I went to the locker room, geared up, and got ready to take down some bad guys.

Enough. It would be enough.

It had to be.

———

"CHECK IN EVERY FIVE MINUTES," Hannah said, strapping her knife to her thigh.

I nodded, making sure the earpiece was secure.

We had a two-mile dead run to the house where the deal was supposed to take place, but we were used to the exertion. We couldn't risk our vehicle being spotted, so whatever gear we needed, we carried. Whatever support we required, whatever backup we might need, was on us.

That was why it was absolutely critical we trusted our teammates.

That was why it had hurt so fucking much to find out that Jack hadn't had our backs.

That was why this thing with Leo, this . . . I hesitated to say it, because it hurt. But while I might have had fantasies, I also had realities. I didn't lie to myself, and that's why I forced myself to think the word. Disgust. Leo was *disgusted* by me.

He'd probably recognized I was pining after him, had mistaken his friendship for more, and was doing us both a kindness by making that clear.

Except his so-called *kindness* felt more like disdain. Like disgust and . . . well, it felt like shit.

Perhaps, he'd decided it was the best way to keep me at a distance, so I stopped the pining, stopped the fantasies, stopped everything except for embracing reality and understanding that nothing would ever happen with us.

Maybe—

This was not the time for this.

We had to be teammates. We were on a mission. We needed to focus; that was the most important thing. I'd prove to him— no, to *myself*, that he wasn't more than a friend, and we'd get on with our lives, our job. I'd get some fucking self-respect back, and all would be right in the world.

"Everyone aware of the second rendezvous point in case we get into trouble?" Hannah asked, shrugging into her backpack.

"Yes," I said, along with everyone else. I secured my bag's clip across my chest.

"Good," she murmured, pocketing the SUV's keys. We

didn't need them, not when the ignition was keyed to our biometrics. If we got into trouble, any one of us could operate the vehicle.

I rolled my shoulders, adjusted my pack, forced a smile, and gave it to the whole team, pretending like Leo hadn't eviscerated me in the conference room, that I wasn't hurting inside and feeling too fucking vulnerable right at this moment. Because maybe if I pretended enough, it would be true. Maybe the rending would heal, and I could . . . I don't know. Stop hurting?

Probably unlikely, given my past.

But a girl had to dream, right?

Focus.

Right.

I made myself meet his eyes, even as I braced myself for him to jump away again, to bolt from me and my "disgusting" presence. He didn't, however, just looked down at me, some unreadable emotion in his gaze. Perfect. Just teammates, see? Exactly what I needed.

An inhale. More shoring. There. *Good.*

"Ready for your first mission, rookie?" I asked lightly, my smile turning genuine.

We could do this. *I* could do this.

"Yup."

A sharp, short sound that had the whole team glancing up from their last-minute preparations.

And then he took a deliberate step away from me.

I sucked in a breath, the shoring and supports I'd erected scattering like fucking toothpicks.

He turned his stare to the trees, a muscle twitching in his jaw.

Something cold buried itself in my heart. Twisted when I faced forward, when I looked away from him, when I saw Hannah and Lily exchange a glance. A *pitying* glance. Inhaling through my nose, I embraced that hurt, let the rage fuel me. I rolled my shoulders again. "Let's go," I said, and took off in the direction of the house.

My feet were silent as I ran, my teammates' feet equally as quiet, and though my heart rate accelerated, my breathing increasing even as I made sure to make my inhalations and exhalations remain as soundless as possible.

But with each step, I grew less aware of my surroundings—dumbass, because that was a stupid fucking move for a KTS agent—and more aware of that stake in my heart, that bitterness festering. Every time the sole of my boot hit the ground, I saw that pitying look. Every time the other collided with the dirt, I remembered Leo lurching away from me. I remembered "Buddy," and the kiss on my thigh, the sharp words.

Over and over and *over* again.

So many times that when I'd finished those two miles, that icy anger had grown, had covered me from head to toe, and I knew there was no going back from it.

I drew to a stop near the edge of the clearing, the house visible just through the trees, felt my teammates come up next to me.

"That was some pace," Linc murmured, resting a hand on a tree trunk, sweat gleaming on his forehead as he caught his breath. His gaze studied mine, as though searching for some answer to a question.

I deliberately looked away, knew that would be answer enough. He was too insightful to not have picked up on what was happening between Leo and me. I cleared my throat. "Let's get into position." The sun had nearly set, and the shadows were growing heavy, allowing us enough cover to sneak closer to the house. We needed to be in position soon in order to avoid disrupting the deal.

"Jesse's right," Hannah said. "Let's go." She squeezed my arm but didn't meet my eyes as she moved by me, signaling to Lily and Linc to follow.

That anger grew, stayed with me as I watched them move into position.

They were liquid night, darting across the back yard, disappearing inside the rickety, abandoned house that appeared ready to fall down around itself. I knew from the video and photos Hannah and Lily had taken during recon that the downstairs was broken up into three rooms—a kitchen, a small living room, and a dining area. A bathroom was there as well, though the walls had long since fallen down, leaving just the toilet and the sink in the middle of the space. Upstairs had two bedrooms and another bathroom, though these walls were still erect. But it was the actual staircase itself that was something out of a horror flick, its banister broken and jagged in places, more treads missing than present, the serrated, wooden edges like hundreds of tiny knives.

More perks of being a secret agent.

Increased risk of getting slivers.

Really big slivers.

"They're good," Leo murmured.

His voice sparked my fury anew. It was the voice of the Leo I knew, the man I'd thrown knives with, the man who'd been my friend. It was *not* the voice of the man from the conference room, from the clearing by the SUV, and . . . it was fucking whiplash.

Friend to asshole to friend.

What the fuck was I supposed to do with that?

All it did was make me defensive, make me want to lash out at him. Except—I sighed—we were on a mission, and that came first. As we watched our teammates slip through the shadows and move into position, I knew I needed to bury the urge, to focus on the task at hand.

"*Really* good," Leo murmured with a grin, and then he bumped my shoulder with his.

He. Touched. *Me.*

Something inside me snapped.

I needed to get away from him. I needed space. I needed to shove down, to lock up, to put all my efforts into pretending. I couldn't do that if he was *touching* me. "I'll take the front watch," I said, taking a step in that direction.

"Jess—" Leo snagged my hand, frowning. "It's too dang—"

Something else snapped inside me.

Maybe it was the concern in his eyes, his worry about me getting hurt when he had sliced me repeatedly with an emotional blade over the last few hours. Maybe he didn't mean it. Maybe there was shit going on with him, and that had caused him to react poorly.

But I wasn't a fucking punching bag.

I yanked out my knife, pressed it to his throat. "Don't finish that statement if you—"

His eyes sparked, and quick as a flash, he'd gripped my wrist, snatched my knife out of my grip. "Want to live?" he asked archly, tossing it back to me.

"Yes," I muttered, catching the knife. "And no, it's not too fucking dangerous. I'm an agent, same as you."

He stepped close. "*I'll* take the front watch. You stay here."

"Where there's little risk of action?" I rolled my eyes, gestured at my body, strong and fit and designed for exactly this kind of work. "I can take care of myself," I reminded him. "I've trained for this as long as you have."

"My job is to have your back."

"Then do it," I hissed, clenching my fingers on my knife, barely resisting the urge to have it at his throat again. "And stop fucking talking so I can do *my* job." I narrowed my eyes. "I'm taking the front watch, and if you have a problem with that, you can just shut the fuck up about it and complain to Hannah later."

He lifted his hands, as though in surrender, muttered, "What's crawled up your ass?"

What had crawled up *my* ass? *My* ass?

"Arrogant, asshole men," I snapped.

A brow rose. A sardonic grin twisted his lips. "And I'm guessing you consider me one of those?"

My nostrils flared. I would not stab him. I *would* not.

I shoved my blade into its sheath. "If the shoe fits." I tossed my head. "And you might as well add misogynistic mother-fucker to it. Just in case you need some flavor or maybe some lovely little sparkles of decoration," I added, fluttering my fingers through the air. "It goes perfectly with your outfit."

Suddenly, I was pinned against the tree, his hard body against mine. "Bullshit," he snapped, his mouth a millimeter from mine, hot breath puffing against my lips. "I am *not* a misogynist."

My breathing wasn't the least bit steady, especially when his hand dropped to my hip, his chest to mine.

"Just a cruel bastard then," I spat. "One who enjoys hurting people."

Something crossed his face—fury, pain? No, it was definitely fury. His fingers clenched tighter on my hip. "I love women."

"*That's* the part you heard?" I gritted out.

His breath painted my lips. "That's the part that's untrue. I'm not a misogynist."

"But you *are* a cruel bastard?" I asked.

"Yes," he agreed without preamble. "I've never had a problem with women, you know that."

I sniffed, rolled my eyes. "So long as they're not your equals?"

Fury drifted across his face. "Take that back."

"No." I shoved at his chest, but short of stabbing him, I had no means of escape. He had me pinned, my back to the tree, his heavy body blocking me in, his grip on my hip nearly unbreakable because . . . I didn't *want* to hurt him.

Even though I wanted to stab him.

Yes, I was perfectly aware that the series of thoughts didn't make one lick of sense.

No, I still didn't stab him.

"You're an asshole," I said instead, venom in every word. "And a shitty fucking friend."

His nostrils flared, green eyes darkening, and I braced myself for more sharp words.

But instead, they were soft.

And surprising.

"I know," he whispered.

His head dropped and suddenly, his breath was on my skin, his nose running slowly up my throat.

"I *know*," he repeated, inhaling.

Goose bumps on my skin, a shiver along my nape.

His head came up, and his lips . . . were right there.

My pulse galloped in my veins, my fingers went from pushing him away to clutching him closer.

I watched his eyes change, knew the moment he'd decided to kiss me.

And I wanted that? I didn't? I—

"Check in," our earpieces blared.

Leo jumped back.

I swallowed hard, tapped my earpiece to turn on the mic as I stepped away from the tree. "Moving to take the front watch right now. Leo is on the rear."

"Here," Leo murmured, and I heard his voice behind me and in my ear.

The rest of the team checked in as I kept moving.

"Jess," he said softly before I was out of earshot. "Wait, I—"

I didn't turn around.

CHAPTER ELEVEN

Leo

I HAD APPROXIMATELY two minutes to berate myself after Jess murmured into the earpiece, "In position," before she said, "Approaching vehicle."

Then I was locking down my emotions, transitioning into Warrior Mode.

And still feeling like the biggest asshole on the planet.

Probably because I'd gotten into the habit of calling it Warrior Mode. Or maybe because I'd been an unforgivable asshole to Jess, and I deserved her vitriol and fury. I'd pushed her away, hurt her, and I'd done a damned good job of it.

Sighing, because my palm still burned remembering the feel of Jesse's hip, I moved further into position, scanning my surroundings, listening for the sound of tires, shifting slightly when I heard the crunch of gravel so I could get a better view of the front porch.

Two men closed their car doors, the sound loud in the quiet of the night, their carefree voices reaching my ears.

Not nervous.

Not on alert.

Hopefully, that meant they hadn't been tipped off.

They sat on the top step of the porch, completely relaxed, chatting about . . . my ears strained to hear, ". . . and then she reached down my pants and just grabbed my dick."

"Bullshit," Lily muttered into the earpiece. "That little shit has never been touched by a woman."

"I agree," Linc said lightly.

Hannah snorted, murmured "There's no accounting for taste. The *little shit* could absolutely have gotten laid."

"Because some women are gluttons for punishment," Jess whispered.

I hated her tone.

It slid right through my Warrior Mode, puncturing it as effectively as a pin to a balloon.

I wanted to run to the front of the house, to sprint to Jesse's position and apologize, explain that I was fucked up in my head and had a hard-on for her, and I knew I couldn't act on anything because we were friends and teammates, and I'd done that before, and it had all gone to shit, and I couldn't be responsible for—

A second car pulled up.

The pair on the porch grew quiet.

Two more car doors slammed. Two more young men strolled up the walkway, leaning against the wobbly railing on the porch.

"Do you have them?" One of the guys sitting asked.

My body went on full alert.

The new pair nodded, and the one on the left went to the rear of the beat-up sedan. He popped the trunk, pulled out . . . a large blue and white cooler. I frowned, pulled out my binoculars to look closer at what appeared to be an ordinary cooler.

"I thought it would be . . . bigger," Lily murmured.

Me, too.

I used my binoculars to scan the surroundings, searching for something else, some*one* else. My spine was prickling, telling me we were missing something.

"Who's got eyes on the cooler?"

There was a pause and then a whisper of sound, a tree shifting just barely in the distance. "I do," Jess said.

We waited, eyes trained on the man carrying the cooler to the porch.

He plunked it on the ground, tugged open the lid.

"Yes!" one of the original pair said.

"Raided my dad's house," the man—no, the boy, I was starting to realize, said. Not a slender adult, but the lanky lines of a teenager. No, this wasn't right. *None* of this was right.

The boys reached into the cooler, pulled out cans that shone bright silver in the moonlight. Beer.

"Jesse?" Hannah asked.

"More of the same," she replied. "Trunk's empty, too."

"Leo?" Hannah asked. "See anything?"

"Nothing back here."

"Linc? The other vehicle."

A pause, shadows moving on the opposite side of the SUV. "Nothing."

"We wait," Hannah said.

I nodded, though she couldn't see me, and watched as the boys drank their beers, as they reached in for seconds, and then thirds, drifting around to the back yard to sit on a stump and talk about all the girls they'd had—or were pretending they'd had. I kept an eye on them after they'd returned for a fourth beer each, then another on Jess as she silently disabled the cars' engines.

They could barely make it to the cooler; they wouldn't be driving home.

Later, after the beers were gone and they'd returned to the back yard, sprawled out on the grass and drinking toasts to the stars, I kept watch as Linc searched through their vehicles.

And found nothing.

No weapons. No trackers. No KTS-grade tech.

Just fucking Puka shell necklaces, a keychain for the local high school, and a pair of crusty underwear.

Boys were fucking gross.

We'd mobilized an elite unit of secret agents to watch high schoolers get drunk off cheap beer and find crusty underwear.

I loved my fucking job.

That was sarcasm, not that anyone residing in my brain could possibly miss it. Not that anyone was residing *in* my brain. Not that . . . I was making any sense. And *that* was solely the responsibility of the woman I could just occasionally glimpse in the shadows near the gravel driveway.

I was in knots because of Jess.

Gripping tight to my focus, I waited with the rest of the team, watching the boys until they passed out, still looking up at the stars. Lily checked on them, rolling them over onto their sides to make sure they were alive and wouldn't choke on their own vomit, if it came to that. It was a far step further to ensuring the horny fuckers' lives than I probably would have taken—

Then again, we all knew I was an asshole.

As Lily was playing mom, Hannah checked the cooler, and no surprise to any of us, found nothing. Linc checked the cars again. Also found nothing. Jesse and I combed the woods.

A big fat *nothing.*

But still we stayed at the house, watching as the first rays of sun drifted up in the sky, brightening it to reds and oranges before we decided to call this a bust and head out.

Either the information Jesse had pulled was inaccurate— unlikely, I knew based on her commitment and the amount of time she'd spent vetting the data—or the weapons deal had been derailed by a bunch of high school dumbasses wanting to drink their Thursday night away. Bottom line, it wasn't happening today, wasn't happening here, and it would be best to go back to base and sort through the failure.

Dark circles smudged the skin beneath Jesse's eyes as we ran back to the car, but I could have gotten a bead on her exhaustion without even looking at her. It radiated in the space between us, heavy waves that crashed into me over and over again. Even so, she set the pace for the rest of us, somehow even more brutal than it had been on the way over. My ribs cramped. My thighs felt weak as hell. My lungs were filled with shards of glass.

But I kept pace beside her regardless, deliberately ignoring the dirty look she shot me.

I knew I needed to apologize.

I didn't have the words, and this wasn't the place. But I needed to anyway.

We paused in the clearing where we'd parked the SUV, chests heaving, Lily, Linc, and Hannah not far behind us but still in the tree line.

I opened my mouth, my apology on the tip of my tongue.

Jesse glanced at me, her skin gilded in the early morning sunshine, those freckles I wanted to count dotted across her nose and cheeks.

"I—"

Her gaze slid by me.

Her eyes went wide.

Faster than I could turn around to assess the threat, Jess had knocked me to the ground, thrown her body over mine like a shield.

"Down!" she shouted.

I heard a *pop*, and—

She hissed.

Her body jerked.

And then blood began gushing out of her throat.

CHAPTER TWELVE

Jesse

WE EMERGED FROM THE TREES, stepped into the clearing, my heart pounding, lungs sawing.

The SUV was in front of us, and I wanted nothing more than to just get into it and get the fuck back to base. Not only because of Leo but because of the fucking weapons exchange . . . or the lack of one anyway.

Where had I gone wrong?

I'd researched. I'd re-researched. I'd run all the details by everyone and—

We'd spent the night surveilling teenagers.

My fault. *My* goddamned fault.

Leo spun to face me, his lips parting, and I braced for more vitriol, for more of that push-pull, whiplash of friend to enemy to friend—

A flash of black in the trees behind him.

I narrowed my eyes, stared across the clearing, just to the left of the SUV, and saw the movement again. Movement that was happening in the wrong direction of my teammates, the build of a man much burlier than the lean strength of Linc, shaped more like Leo.

Except, Leo was in front of me.

And I knew.

The world was about to go to shit.

The man in the trees raised his arm. I saw the gun and—

I moved before I even processed what I was doing, grabbing Leo's shoulders, sweeping out with my foot, taking us both to the ground, as I shouted, "Down!" to warn Linc and Hannah and Lily, who were just coming up behind us.

Leo was below me, his eyes wide, his lips forming words, but . . . too late.

I heard the gun discharge, felt the sharp bite of pain, the warm gush of blood.

But Leo was okay.

I reached for my own weapon, raised it and fired off a few quick shots to buy us some time. Then Leo had flipped us, his hand gripping my throat tightly enough that I gagged, his other holding his gun, firing rapidly.

"Move!" I heard in my earpiece.

Hannah's voice.

The rest of our team laid down cover fire, and I scrambled to my feet or maybe it was more that Leo hauled me up, and then we were sprinting for the tree line. I was dizzy, stumbling, but we made it the ten feet, bullets whizzing around us. It wasn't a warzone, didn't have the explosions and screams that some-times still made up my nightmares.

Instead, it was surprisingly quiet outside of the rapports of the gunfire, the hissed orders from Hannah in my earpiece. Whoever was out there already knew our positions, so there wasn't a huge benefit to keeping quiet, but panic and the yelling never brought anything good. And we were better than that, I thought, fighting to keep my eyes open, knowing I wouldn't be a help to anyone if I slipped into unconsciousness, so I held tight to my awareness, focused on my surroundings.

We'd taken up cover behind a fallen tree, Hannah and Lily on either side of us, their backs pressed to thick trunks that would protect them.

Linc was already there, kneeling next to me, his medic kit out, and I winced when he dumped clotting agent—KTS's special sauce for just this situation—into my wound then began wrapping a bandage with even more of the compound embedded into the gauze, yanking it tight enough that I had to force back another gag.

"Eyes?" he ordered, flashing his light quickly through mine.

"I'm good," I said, my voice more rasp than smooth, starting to sit up. "How many—"

Leo's hand dropped to my shoulder. "Stay down," he hissed.

"Fuck off," I rasped, shoving my elbows beneath me, dislodging the hand, but another took its place.

My eyes went to Linc's.

"Give the agent time to work," he murmured, expression grave and telling me just how serious the wound was. "Just a few minutes."

I sucked in a breath that felt like barbed wire, but I nodded, leaned back against the tree. My head was swimming anyway, and I could use the time to bolster my strength.

Linc squeezed my shoulder once then crouched next to me, gun in hand, gaze tracking the targets on the far side.

How many were there?

More than one, that was for sure.

The bullets continued to collide with the trees, a rapid *thunk* and *plink* that spoke to more than a handful. They were coming from three—four?—directions.

So not quite outgunned, but close. Especially since we didn't have an infinite amount of ammo.

I needed to help.

Leo's eyes were sweeping back and forth through our surroundings. Linc's following suit. I kept my gaze behind us as

I swapped out my nearly empty clip for a full one, sliding a bit higher and waiting for my head to stop swimming, knowing that if I had to sit here, the least I could do was keep an eye on our backs.

"Good?" Hannah asked, her stare meeting mine for just a heartbeat after I waited the requisite few minutes for the clotting agent to work then sat up a little further.

"Good," I repeated, despite the spinning head, the aching throat, the blood drying on my skin.

"Backup's en route," she said. "Ten minutes."

Ten minutes. I could hold out for ten minutes, even as my vision swam and my hands shook, the pain continuing to creep in.

Nothing behind, bullets still raining down in front of us, but the frequency slowing.

I risked a glanced over my shoulder, ignoring the agony that tore through me with the action, squinting to try and spot whoever the fuck had decided to shoot at us on the far side of the clearing. My bleeding had slowed, the clotting agent working, but I'd lost enough blood that it was getting harder and harder to stay focused as the minutes ticked by. I could see the SUV riddled with bullet holes—or at least dents, the bulletproof metal doing its job. Behind it, across the tree line, I could see the men who were firing at us peeling off, disappearing deeper into the shadows of the tree line, as though they knew backup was coming and couldn't afford to be captured.

They would take the chance to eliminate a team but didn't want to be caught.

There had to be another traitor, or they had been watching us and knew this was the best place for an ambush, or the whole weapons deal had been a fucking trap, and I'd walked my team right into it.

"Stop."

A sharp word, a tone from Leo I was becoming familiar with.

But this time, it was paired with a gentle squeeze of my shoulder, a soft murmur, "It's not your fault." I glanced up, saw the lines of Leo's jaw clenched taut. Emerald eyes on mine, soft in their depths despite the gunshots still plinking around us. "It's not," he repeated, a muscle twitching, his lips pressed flat. Then he lifted his head, focused across the clearing.

I tore my gaze away from him, keeping watch on our backs, smelling the damp earth, feeling the sun starting to shine on my skin. The latter two sensory images weren't helpful, didn't bring anything except for distractions.

Woozy.

I was so damned woozy.

Shadows in my vision, this time not giving away the enemy, but rather my unconscious brain trying to yank me under.

I fought it, gripped my gun in both hands.

"Clip?" Linc asked, pulling me out of the fog.

I tore open the Velcroed pocket on my thigh, yanked one out for him.

"Thanks."

Knowing I should be the one thanking our medic for helping me refocus, to stay conscious, to pull out energy from somewhere and stay awake, I filed my gratitude away to be given during a later time.

The minutes ticked by.

Staying conscious got increasingly difficult.

Then there was the glorious sound of SUVs, of another voice in our earpieces, one that I recognized and respected.

"Okay, Cinderellas," Laila said. "We're here. Get your asses to the carriages before we all turn into pumpkins."

"Watch yourself," Hannah warned. "Four unfriendlies at nine o'clock."

"Roger that," Laila said, just as a pair of black SUVs tore into the clearing kicking up rocks and glass. They spun to a sliding stop, facing out toward the exit, a bulletproof barrier between us and those on the other side. A moment later, the rear driver's side doors flew open on both vehicles.

"Go, Jesse," Hannah ordered.

Knowing my team wouldn't leave until the injured—until *I* —was safe, I pushed up onto my feet, summoned strength from somewhere, and ran.

Even though my head spun.

Even though my legs felt like they would give out.

I clenched my gun in both hands, leaped out from the trees, and sprinted toward the SUV.

A wavering, faltering sprint, bullets pinging around me— from behind me as cover, from in front of me coming out of the opposite tree line, from the SUV as Laila and her team brought enough firepower to protect us.

I made it to the SUV, Leo behind me a moment later, shoving me inside, Linc a heartbeat after him.

The door slammed.

"Hannah," I said. "Lily—"

"The other SUV," Linc said.

We accelerated, more rapidly than I anticipated, and I was thrown back against the seat, hissing out a breath when the SUV shot forward. Leo's hand came up to the back of my head, fingers threading into my ponytail.

"Easy," he murmured, fingertips pressed gently on my scalp. "We're safe."

And that was the moment I lost my fight.

I slumped, unconsciousness tugging me under.

CHAPTER THIRTEEN

Leo

"SHE'S OUT," I said to Linc.

He reached over, took her pulse, gave her a quick once-over. It probably would have been better if I had let the medic sit next to Jesse, but watching her stumble across the clearing, blood clinging to the black of her uniform, staining the porcelain of her neck crimson, seeping through the white of the bandage Linc had secured around her throat, while bullets flew all around her, had made my heart seize.

Hannah had thankfully given the order for us to peel off and follow, and not a moment too soon, because I had already been pushing off the ground, readying to run after her, to scoop her in my arms, and haul her to safety.

It hadn't taken much to catch up.

She'd been slow and unsteady.

But also strong.

Because she'd reached the vehicle, had been readying to haul herself inside before I could help her in, help her to slide across the seat, even as she was somehow still alert, those blue eyes scanning me, scanning Linc with a weighty, concerned gaze before asking about Lily and Hannah.

Strength. Beauty.

I didn't understand how they'd ever been separate in my head.

Because as I sat beside her, my fingers in her hair, her eyes closed, lashes dark half-moons on her cheeks, I knew I had never seen anything more beautiful.

———

I WAS SITTING beside her bed in the infirmary, Lily, Hannah, and Linc beside me.

I'd carried her here from the car, watching as Linc and his woman, Olive, had checked her over, cleaning the gunshot wound—miraculously a through and through without hitting anything major—giving her a blood transfusion, and stitching her up.

Now, we were waiting for her to wake up.

I was silently going over the mission notes, trying to find something unusual with the information that Jess had pulled. But as I reread page after page, it all seemed normal, it all seemed to point to that location, that date, the KTS-grade weapons up for grabs.

So, maybe it truly *was* just a bunch of teenagers fucking up and stepping on our toes.

Or maybe we had another traitor in our midst.

I hoped for the first, knew it was the second.

But all I *did* know for sure was that nothing about the material Jesse had gathered pointed to her having done anything wrong. We'd all re-checked her work, both now that we were in the debriefing stage and previously before we'd gone on the mission in the first place. Every single duck was in a row.

And then it appeared that every duck had decided to

fucking go wild, zipping this way and that, refusing to march in normal, single-file lines.

This had been happening again and again *and* again.

Ever since we'd found out about Daniel and his treachery, about Jack and his betrayal, things had been slowly unfurling.

Missions fucked.

Weapons missing.

Assets—both monetary and physical—disappearing.

Details and locations of our bases, our agents, leaked, putting everyone at risk, and causing agents to get hurt . . . to die.

Linc's phone buzzed, and his gaze flicked down at the screen, reading before slipping it back into his pocket.

"Olive?" Lily asked.

He nodded. "Dominic has a parent-teacher conference."

Dominic was the kid, well teenager, really, that Olive and Linc had taken in after he'd helped Olive, at much risk to himself, during another mission gone FUBAR. His mother had been swept up into the net of deceit that was Daniel, and the poor kid had been surviving on his own. Until Olive had made him hers.

Now he was part of KTS and would be until it was safe for him to return to the real world.

"Go," Hannah said. "We'll stay here until—" She broke off with a wince when her own cell buzzed. "Laila," she said, tugging it out of her pocket. Her gaze drifted to Lily's, to mine. "They need us to debrief her team."

Lily stood, nodded.

I remained sitting. "They don't need all three of us. You guys go. I'll stay here in case Jess wakes up and needs anything."

Hannah's expression was so locked down that I couldn't read anything.

But after a moment, she nodded and pushed to her feet, followed Lily and Linc toward the door.

"Leo." I glanced up, saw she'd stopped just inside the doorway. I watched as the wooden panel slowly began to close. She caught it just before it clicked shut. "You hurt her again, and you're off my fucking team."

Then the door was opening and closing again.

Only this time, it shut without anyone stopping it.

And then it was just me and Jess.

And my heavy-ass guilty conscience.

CHAPTER FOURTEEN

Jesse

I woke with pain tearing down my throat, my limbs heavy and my mouth dry.

But I was on something soft.

A bed, I realized, managing to open my eyelids, even though they felt like they'd had concrete blocks tied to my eyelashes. I blinked a few times until my vision cleared enough for me to see my blankets—someone must have retrieved them from my room, since I was clearly in the infirmary—had been tucked around me. The small TV mounted on the far wall was on, but without any sound, the scene from some action movie making the shadows dance along the walls.

I slowly took stock of my body, moving my toes, my fingers, flexing and straightening my feet.

Other than exhaustion tearing through me, I was fine.

"Here."

Leo's voice made me jump and then bite back a curse when a bolt of red-hot pain shot down my throat.

He winced, slowly raised the bed so I could drink. "Sorry." He held out the cup, or rather pressed it into my fingers, then lifted my hand so that the rim of the glass was against my lips. I took a huge swallow, felt some of the fire in my throat extinguish. Then continued drinking until the cup was drained. "More?" he asked.

I shook my head, rasped, "What are you doing here?"

"What do you remember?"

Closing my eyes, I thought back. The bullets and hiding behind the fallen tree. Pain and blood. Cold words and lurching away and . . . even more pain.

"How many stitches?" I countered.

"Only ten," he said. "Six in the front. Four in the back. Linc and Olive cleaned you up once we got back to base. You'll be out of commission for a few days, mainly because of the blood transfusion."

"How much blood?"

"Two bags."

I started to nod. Stopped because it fucking hurt then settled on a shrug. Not the worst, I'd had. Not the best.

He got up, poured me another glass of water, pressed it into my hand again. "How long was I out?"

"Not long." A glance at his watch. "Six hours."

Again, not the worst I'd had. Not the best.

Another shrug as I continued to sip the water. Each swallow was painful, but it was a good pain, smoothing over the rough edges, easing the ache. By the time I finished the second glass, I felt a whole lot more human.

"You had me worried there for a second," Leo murmured, smoothing back my hair.

Slowly, carefully, I slid away from him.

I couldn't have him touching me, speaking to me. Not like that. Not soft and gentle and with affection and kindness. Not after what he'd said, what he'd done in response to my words, my touch.

Not after all the whiplash.

He drew his hand back but didn't leave, just sank onto the edge of the bed and stared at me. His eyes were . . .

No.

I wouldn't read anything into that expression.

"Why are you here?" I snapped.

An abrupt question, my tone even more so. Harsh. Brittle. Cold.

A flicker of something else in his eyes. Something I didn't want to look too closely at because it was probably hurt, and I didn't want—no, I didn't *care* that I'd hurt him. Even if there was a tendril of guilt winding through me.

Leo was a friend. I didn't like to hurt my friends.

Except . . . he hadn't acted like one, and I was too raw inside to worry about him right at this moment anyway.

"Jess, baby, I—"

I turned my head away, ignoring the way it yanked on my stitches, the fire it wrought on my throat. "You should go."

His fingers brushed my jaw, the lightest feather of a touch. One I'd dreamed about for an eternity, and one that was more painful than my injury.

"Don't," I whispered, barely able to resist jerking away.

Another brush of his fingers, the calluses on their tips making me shiver. "I'm so—"

To my horror, I felt a tear escape, slide down my cheek, a burning trail of shame.

He caught it with his thumb.

"Jess, I—"

"I can't do this right now," I said miserably, my gaze on the TV on the far side of the room. I wanted to be in my quarters, surrounded by my things. It probably shouldn't make any difference. I didn't have a lot of belongings, nothing much outside of clothes and weapons and tech that I needed to live my life. There hadn't been room for knickknacks in my garbage bag of clothing that I'd brought from home to home. No posters or artwork. No trophies or medals or stuffed toys. No room for them. No one to buy them for me.

But my rooms here were mine. They were comfortable and safe and—

Leo intruded on that. "I need to—"

"I can't hear it," I whispered. "I can't hear *anything*. I'm too —" I cut myself off before I revealed exactly how wounded I was . . . and I wasn't talking about the one on my neck. Sighing, I closed my eyes, felt another tear fall.

He caught it again.

I jerked my head away, gasped at the pain, eyes stinging, the tears coming faster. "Go," I said miserably.

"I'm—"

Rolling to my side, I gave him my back, kept my lids slammed shut, ignoring him, ignoring the pain.

A sigh.

Then, "I'm sorry."

I didn't reply, not when that apology had buried itself like a knife in my middle, taking my breath along with it. I didn't move. It didn't change anything. *It didn't.* After what felt like an eternity, I heard a rustle of fabric, felt the bed jostle slightly as he pushed himself up to his feet. Then footsteps leading away.

The *click* of the knob turning.

The shift of air when the door opened and closed.

Only then did I allow the rest of the tears to fall, the sobs to come. It hurt—my wound, my heart. My memories and present and future, all swirled together, tearing through me. Those feelings of not belonging, of not being worthy, were quickly followed by rage—at myself, at everyone else . . . but mostly at myself because I just never seemed to find a way to fit in.

I hated that I tried my damnedest to reduce myself, to get quiet and small, just so I could find my place somewhere, only for it to not really work anyway.

I hated that I was . . . me.

And I hated that I had even had that thought in the first

place. I should love myself, my giant Raggedy Ann ass, my strong shoulders and arms and legs. I *should*. I knew I should.

But . . . I just didn't have it in me in that moment.

Not after the injury. Not after the letdown of the mission. Not after Leo.

Right now, I just wanted to wrap myself in my misery and cry until I didn't have any more tears.

The bed dipped again, and before I could process what was happening, warm arms wrapped around me, tugging me back against a muscular chest, Leo's soft words in my ear. "It's all right," he murmured. "You're safe now. Nothing else bad is going to happen."

He was trying to be comforting.

He only made me feel worse.

My tears came faster, torn out of my lungs, painful in my throat and ears, the sounds broken and horrible and yet something I had no control of stopping.

Because I'd been shot.

Because my heart hurt, my fantasies had been stomped to dust.

Because . . . I wasn't safe here, not in his arms, not when he might send sharp barbs my way again, not when he might make me feel even smaller than I already made myself, not when he might stomp on me again.

I struggled against him, shoving at his chest.

But he was stronger than me and bigger than me, and I wasn't really capable of any *true* struggle, not when I couldn't catch my breath, not when my throat was wounded, not when my heart was sliced so deeply.

"I'm sorry," he said. "I'm sorry you got hurt. I'm sorry you did that for me. I'm sorry that I was such a dick. I'm sorry . . ."

He kept talking, but I tuned him out.

Apologies.

Easy words.

But I'd been taught often enough to not believe them. I

might cling to fantasies, but despite that kernel of hope, I'd always known those imaginings weren't real. I dealt in actions and reality, because when I'd dared to dream the slightest bit—spending the last few nights thinking about Leo outside my door, his mouth on my thigh, him leaning close before we'd been interrupted by Hannah, remembering the careful way he'd tucked my hair behind my ear, how his fingers had brushed mine and made me shiver—when I'd dreamed for one moment he might actually be interested in me (*me!*), I'd opened myself up to this agony.

Embarrassment and disappointment and a dose of leftover adrenaline.

It was a deadly combination.

Especially with his arms around me, with his soft words, with the weak seeping into my bones and keeping me there.

He held me like I was more than a friend.

Wiped my tears like a lover.

Spoke my name as though it were cherished.

More fantasy.

Exhaustion rippled over me like a tidal wave, and blackness tugged me under.

CHAPTER FIFTEEN

Leo

She was asleep in my arms.

She fit . . . perfectly.

And I was reminded all over again how fucking much of an asshole I was. I'd wiped her tears, held her back to my front, and listened to her cry herself into unconsciousness.

I'd like to think it was adrenaline let-down from the wound.

I knew differently.

She was hurting because of me.

Because I'd been doing things with her when I shouldn't, keeping her close, making her think . . . I could give her something more than I could.

Even if I were finally removed enough from denial to understand that I could never look at her again strictly as a friend, as a teammate. I'd glimpsed the beauty of her I'd been too dumb to see before, and I could never go back from it, not now.

But I also couldn't go forward.

Couldn't claim her as mine.

Because . . . I didn't *do* that anymore. Not since—

I closed my eyes. Not since blood had poured between my

fingers, dripped down my arms, turning the earth crimson, leaving stains on my hands that never could be washed away.

Despite all that, in that moment, I couldn't let Jess go.

Not when she rolled over in my arms, her limp body to mine, her warm breath on the bare skin of my throat.

Not when nothing had ever felt more right.

She shifted in her sleep, snuggled closer.

I drew her nearer, held her tighter, and knew that this was the one night that I would allow myself.

Then I would go back . . . to friends, to teammates, and if neither of those things worked, to nothing at all.

CHAPTER SIXTEEN

Jesse

WARMTH WOKE ME.

Smothered me.

My throat was on fire. My chest ached.

My eyes didn't want to open.

But then they did, and my sharp inhale of breath made tears prickle. A slow inhale, an even slower exhale, steadying my heartbeat . . . because I was in Leo's arms, pressed to his chest, his breath ruffling my hair, his spicy scent in my nose.

And it meant nothing.

Light flickered over the ceiling, shadows from the movie still playing in the background.

Exhaustion rippled through me, dragged me down. Every part of me wanted to burrow closer, to live in the fantasy, but I knew that I'd wake up in the morning and Leo would look at me, not the way I hoped for, not like I was the other half of his heart, not like he'd love every part of me, not like—

I meant something.

I froze, lifted my fingers to the bandage, the wound tender but so much less so than it would have been if I didn't have the clotting agent, if Linc hadn't been there to doctor me up. An inch either way, and I could have died.

I could have died feeling this bad about myself.

I could have died thinking that I might never mean something to anyone else, and seriously, how fucked up was that?

What was the point of surviving this long if I was just going to be miserable and alone and always thinking that I wasn't worth something? I thought about Hannah, strong and confident, living a big life that was full of color. I thought about Lily, always finding the humor in a situation, even as she embraced experiences with open arms. They weren't small or quiet. They didn't care if someone didn't like them. They were intrinsically themselves.

And I was so fucking jealous of that.

Because I didn't think *I* knew myself.

"Fuck," I said under my breath, carefully slipping out from Leo's arms and moving through the quiet halls of the base, back to my rooms, letting the door shut behind me as I walked into my bathroom. There, I splashed water on my face, stared at the woman in the mirror.

Haunted.

A stranger.

I was twenty-nine years old, and I'd spent my life being another person, until I didn't even recognize the reflection of myself in the mirror.

Who was I?

Who?

I wanted a simple answer. Funny and smart like Lily. Intense and never backed down like Hannah.

But every adjective that came to mind as I studied myself in the mirror wasn't good. They were all toxic and slicing and, God, was I really going to live the rest of my life like this?

My fingers gripped the edge of the counter, and I hung my head, knowing I couldn't do it. I couldn't live like this, Leo or not. I couldn't be this girl who hated herself any longer. It clawed at me, suffocated me until I felt as though the bandage around my neck was tightening, invisible fingers yanking at it, cutting off my flow of air.

Heart pounding, breaths coming in rapid gusts, I reached for the faucet, needing more cold water, needing a shock of cold to snap me out of this.

My hand bumped the little porcelain soap dish, knocked it to the tile.

"No," I whispered, watching it fall and yet unable to stop it.

The dish shattered, pieces scattering in all directions, and for a moment, I just stared at it, sitting broken and ugly on the white floor. Then I bent, trying to fit the pieces back together, as though it would be fine if I could just grab every shard and force them back together.

Then no one would know.

And that was when *I* knew.

As I stared at the one thing I had from my mother, the one item I'd carried from house to house to house, from base to base, from my old life all the way through to this one, I knew that I'd been broken, the pieces long lost.

Never to be the same again.

Even if I clung to the fantasy of it.

I had to let the fantasy go. But could I? Was I strong enough?

I reached for a shard I hadn't grabbed before, this one having slid beneath the vanity, and hissed when it sliced my finger, bringing the digit up to my mouth and sucking the injury until it stopped stinging.

Then I picked up the remaining pieces and plunked them into the trash can, slivers and chunks and shards, all pointed, all sharp, all able to wound. And I knew it would hurt, I knew it wouldn't be easy.

But I also knew that I couldn't live another moment pretending.

Standing, I stared at my reflection, saw a flicker of the woman I wanted to be—not small, not wounded. I wanted

Lily's humor. I wanted Hannah's take-no-bullshit. I wanted Linc's strength in being heartbroken but then finding the courage to grasp tight to love a second time. I wanted Olive's big heart and easy openness. I wanted Dan's loyalty, Laila's confidence, Ava's perseverance, Ryker's quiet steadiness.

And . . . I wanted to be me.

Now, I just needed to figure out who I was.

CHAPTER SEVENTEEN

Leo

I WOKE to the sound of . . . nothing.

To an empty bed.

It was an instant awareness, one second unconscious, the next with crystal-like clarity.

I was in the infirmary, in the room that Jess had been given. Alone.

I'd slept in her bed, with her in my arms.

I wanted to do that again, do it every night for the rest of my life, albeit in a bigger bed. I wanted to wake with her, even though she wasn't next to me. I wanted a do-over, so I could see what she looked like with morning sunshine on her cheeks, her eyelids slowly peeling back.

But . . . I couldn't.

I just . . . *couldn't.*

Inhaling sharply, I pushed out of the bed, my jeans feeling stiff and uncomfortable, my mouth like it had been home to a forest fire.

I should go back to my rooms, shower, and get to work.

If Jess was up and moving, she would be all right. I should

get out of her space, leave her to her recovery, and put all my energy into finding the fucker who'd shot her. That was the one good thing I could do, the one thing I could salvage from this fucked up situation.

But after I'd made my way through the halls, had hesitated outside my door, I found myself turning and going to hers, seeing that the panel had shut, but not all the way because the lock hadn't engaged, and . . . I was pushing through when the bathroom door opened, and Jess stepped out.

She stopped, hands gripping a towel that was around her breasts and hit mid-thigh, only an inch or two of the pink scar visible below the white cotton. The waterproof bandage still on her neck, standing out sharply in contrast to all that skin, still flushed from the shower. Her gaze came to mine, and the ice in her eyes chipped away something at me.

She'd changed.

Because of me.

"Jess—" I began.

Then found I didn't have any more words left, not when her next action was to drop her towel.

I'd seen her in a swimsuit.

I'd seen her in a bra and underwear.

I'd seen most of her skin . . . and yet, it was as though I'd never seen her. Miles and miles of creamy skin, dotted with freckles, her pink-tipped breasts so fucking gorgeous, and her pussy—I felt my throat seize when I saw the narrow thatch of red hair, the rosy lips glistening, not from desire, but from the shower. She sniffed, derision in her eyes, and spun toward her dresser.

She yanked out a drawer. "I came to a decision last night." She pulled a pair of underwear out and began tugging them on, her ass jiggling and all too grabbable. "I woke up in the middle of the night, in the arms of the man I've fantasized about forever, and I realized that *nothing* is real." She yanked a sports bra out of another drawer, yanked it over her head, covering her breasts with plain white fabric that was no less tempting than her bare skin. Instead, it plumped and brought together, made my fingers itch to run beneath the hem. "Not our friendship." A shirt came next, jerked down so hard I had to bite back a retort for her to be careful. "That only worked when you could put me into a box, one that was perfectly contained and fit into your expectations." Sweats on her long legs. "It was all good until you realized that I have *these.*" She grabbed her breasts through her shirt. "And *this.*" She pointed between her thighs. "But, newsflash, Leo, I've been a woman all along, and I've spent too fucking long making myself small, trying to fit in somewhere—"

She was magnificent, beautiful, and filled with fire.

I reached for her. "Jess—"

She blew by me, striding to the bathroom, where she grabbed a hairbrush and began yanking it through her hair. "And so I woke up in the middle of the night, and I should have been over the moon because the man I've been in love with for fucking *years* was holding me like I was precious."

I went still. "What?"

"I loved you," she said, tossing the hairbrush onto the counter. "Or at least, I thought I did, and then you kissed my thigh and held me like I was important, and I hoped"—her voice broke—"I *wished* that you finally saw me as someone important."

My heart was pounding; my hands trembled.

"And then I realized that if I kept waiting for everyone else to see me as important, then *I* would never see *me* as important."

"Jess," I murmured, taking a step toward her.

She shook her head, stepped back. "I should have been happy, and when I looked over at you, all I felt was this disgust for myself, the disgust you had for me."

Disgust for her?

No.

Not ever.

It was at me, at myself. "I'm not—"

"And all of a sudden, it all made sense," she said, talking over me. "You're never going to make me happy."

Those words were a punch to my gut.

Because I knew she was right.

"So"—she moved to the door, yanked it open—"I want you to go. To go back to your team, to leave me to mine."

"Jesse," I said. "I'm not disgusted with you. I like you. You're my—"

I broke off, because I didn't know *what* she was to me.

And she knew that.

She pointed out the door. "Leave me to my life, Leo."

I swallowed, wanting to say something to convince her to forgive me but knowing there was absolutely nothing I *could* say. Because I hadn't seen her beauty until it had clocked me over the head, and that had hurt her.

I had hurt her.

"I could have died yesterday," she said, when I didn't immediately move. "And all I could think as I was staring at you was that I don't want this to be my life anymore. I'm done with being small and quiet and trying to making sure no one sees me. I'm"—a sigh—"done with *you.*"

I felt like I was the one who'd been shot.

Like all the blood was leaving my body, as though my soul had frozen and someone had taken a hammer to it, shattering it into a million tiny pieces.

But all I could do was nod and walk to the door.

I turned back, studied her face with the freckles I wanted to count, the nose I was desperate to kiss the tip of, the cute, little elven ears.

"I'm sorry," I whispered.

Her eyes darted away. "Goodbye, Leo."

The only thing left to do . . . was to walk out.

So, I did.

CHAPTER EIGHTEEN

Jesse

I DIDN'T KNOW if I felt better or worse after Leo walked out of the room.

Better because I'd finally stood up for myself, that I'd found an inner wealth of fire inside me, and holy hell, had I just stripped down and marched buck naked across the room like it wasn't a big fucking deal? Also, why did that feel so fucking good? To not be ashamed of my body, to actually be able to see the heat I'd seen in his eyes? He'd been attracted to me. Not someone else.

Me.

Me.

I felt a piece inside me slide into place, a hole being filled in chip by chip.

New me could be a badass. New me could be unashamed. New me could be anything that I wanted.

That was what had felt good, I realized.

Not the heat in Leo's eyes, but the confidence in my heart, the conviction that I was doing the right thing.

Even if I had hurt him.

And that was where the worse in the whole better or worse thing came in, and I felt another sliver wiggle its way back into shape. Because even though I'd wanted to be that strong badass who never backed down, I didn't want to be the type of woman who went around hurting people—even if he'd done it first.

Unfortunately, however, in this case, it had to be done.

I'd woken and enjoyed his warm body against mine for a few precious moments, the spicy scent of him in my nose, on my skin, and I'd known I could lie there and continue pretending that everything would be okay.

I could accept the scraps.

I'd be safe and protected and perfect.

Until I got caught up thinking I didn't deserve that protection. Until I looked in the mirror again and found myself unworthy.

Until he cycled back to asshole and made me feel like shit, and I unraveled any progress I'd made in trying to figure out who in the fuck I was.

Until I let him do it because I thought that was the only thing I deserved.

So . . . that was it then.

No more Leo.

No more heads in the clouds and pretending so the puzzle pieces of what everyone wanted fit into the gaps inside me.

Just me.

Only me in my brain, me trying to sort my head out, me trying to figure out the woman I would be going forward.

I'd survived hell, pain, and loss, and being hurt over and over again.

I'd *survived* it.

Now, I could live it.

And Leo would go back to his life, letting me move forward with mine. No more feeling deficient and broken, no more feeling inadequate.

I'd nearly died, and with my nose pressed to Leo's throat,

I'd realized that I would have left nothing behind. Just a shell of a woman who couldn't stand the sight of herself in the mirror.

And so, I was going to finally do something about it.

I'd remember the way Linc looked at Olive, the gentle way he was with her. How he treated her like she was capable and yet something to protect. I'd remember Dan and Ava—both badasses in their own rights, and yet they'd take on the world for each other. I'd remember Laila and Ryker, who built each other up, who sacrificed in turn, who didn't diminish but expanded each other. I'd remember Hannah and Lily and . . . I'd remember me.

Instead of the possibilities in my dreams.

Because even as I thought back of myself with Leo, how I'd behaved during our friendship, how I'd lied to myself about what could be—even before I'd caught a glimpse of his inner asshole—I didn't like it.

My simpering and fantasizing.

My constant inner monologue of not measuring up.

And . . . it was just enough.

I couldn't go on like this, and it was as though by finally getting something that I'd dreamed about—Leo in my bed, Leo holding me like I mattered—I had finally, *finally* realized none of it meant jack shit unless *I* mattered to me first.

Sad it had taken me nearly thirty years to get there.

But I wasn't going back.

No more.

So, as I watched the door close behind Leo, instead of dropping to the floor, curling up in a ball, and crying until I had no more tears, like I really wanted to, I shoved my feet into shoes, scraped my hair into a ponytail, and . . . I got on with my life.

First matter of business?

Finding out who'd put a bullet through my throat.

———

I WAS PATHETICALLY WEAK.

And I didn't mean emotionally for the first time in my life.

I was physically exhausted—the aftereffects of the blood transfusion. Although, I supposed it was also the aftereffects of the emotional night, my vow to myself, letting go of the fantasy of the perfect happily-ever-after with Leo.

Yeah, maybe that, too.

But I was still in my office, a fresh laptop in hand, one I'd gone out and picked up myself from the local electronics store.

No KTS tech. No one working on it except me.

A mobile hotspot. A VPN.

Not the most secure, but the best I could do under the circumstances, especially when it appeared that KTS's mainframe was compromised.

So, I was going to do some sleuthing outside of it.

Hacking wasn't my strong suit, though we'd all been trained with the basics. Sometimes we couldn't bring tech back to base, sometimes we needed to get in it, right then and there, so I was going to do my best and hope that new equipment untouched by anyone else's hands would bring me the missing piece of information we were lacking.

A knock at my door had me glancing up to see Hannah.

"Hi," I said and went back to my keyboard.

"I thought you weren't supposed to be working."

"I know my limits," I told her, using a firm tone that wasn't me, and yet was also completely me, then adding when she looked ready to protest, "Plus, I'm almost done for today."

Silence.

Then I glanced up, hazel eyes boring into mine. "You're different."

I snorted. "Nearly dying would do that to you."

Hannah rolled her eyes. "We've all nearly died enough times for that to hardly come into play," she said, her tone dry. "So tell me, what's really up?"

"I'm done."

Blond brows lifted. "With what?"

I sighed heavily and closed the laptop, knew I could retreat, could continue to hold everything close to my chest. But—another piece plunked home—that wasn't who I wanted to be. I wanted friendships where I actually told the freaking truth. Such a fucking novelty. Even so, I had to force the words out. "Done giving in to that inner voice."

To Hannah's credit, she didn't seem to miss a beat. "The one that tells you you're worthless?"

My eyes widened, and the urge to retreat was real.

Hannah crossed over to my desk, sat on the edge of it. "You think you're the only one with that particular mental asshole, rattling around your brain like a bean in a pail?"

Bean in a pail?

Where did she get these things?

"No," I said, when I got beyond the analogy that was strangely apt. "But, well, I guess that I never thought that you . . ." I trailed off, realizing that I'd not only been judging myself, but that I'd also been judging everyone else. *I* had the biggest pain. *I* was the one who was unworthy. *I*—

Hadn't opened myself up to anyone enough to find commonality in experience.

Emotional experience, that was.

The work part was easy—not that the missions were easy or went off without a hitch. I had the wound in my neck, the scar on my thigh to prove just the opposite. But it was easy to have common experience when we had a collective. Shoot shit. Save people. Root out traitors.

It had always been.

This was different.

This was leaping out of an airplane, hoping my chute opened. This was diving into the dark ocean water to swim to shore. This was . . . being vulnerable.

"My parents disowned me when they found out I was gay." A shrug, as though this were easy for her to talk about, even though the hurt was there in her hazel eyes, in the tone of her voice. "I went from being miserable because I was hiding everything about myself to being miserable because I was alone." A forced smile. "Nothing like the prodigal only child ruining my parents' dreams, right?"

"I'm sorry," I said, reaching across the desk and squeezing her hand, and I found that I could do this, even if it was just a little bit. "If it makes you feel any better, my dad was never more than a sperm donor, and my mom died when I was six, so I was bounced around family until the system stepped in."

She flipped her hand over, so her palm was pressed to mine. "It doesn't," she said simply. "Same as I know it doesn't make you feel good to know we share a sob story."

That much was true.

My eyes lifted to hers. "I thought if I could just be good enough, if I crammed myself into a tiny enough box, then someone would want me."

"I wish that were the case." Hannah squeezed my fingers. "It sure would solve a lot of problems."

That much was true.

But it wasn't.

"I'm done with that."

An approving smile. "I'm proud of you."

Four words I'd never heard before. Four words that shifted more pieces around, jiggling them into proper position.

"How did you . . ." I trailed off.

"What?"

Normally, I would have demurred, gotten quiet, and pretended the question wasn't there. I would have thrown the wall up, so I didn't let anyone in past my carefully constructed barriers. But that wasn't who I wanted to be forever. I *wanted* to be more than that. I wanted to stop feeling like a fucking outsider and to start being part of something.

Which meant that I couldn't retreat.

I needed to press forward. So, I asked the question on my

mind, the one I hoped would give me an answer that would help bolster me. "How did you move on from that?"

Her hazel eyes went serious. "From my parents?"

I nodded.

"I—" A shrug. "Truthfully, I wish that I'd had a magical epiphany about self-worth and that all of a sudden I was fine and happy and strong."

"It didn't work that way?"

Hannah's mouth curved into a rueful smile. "Unfortunately, no."

I sighed.

"What?"

"Because I had my epiphany last night, and I was hoping it would solve everything." Hannah's brows lifted, so I added, "I woke up in the middle of the night and just couldn't stand the person I'd become. It was like my reflection was a pitiful creature I just couldn't be anymore, and . . . I just wanted to be different."

"So, you took a step."

I nodded. "Yeah."

"So, that's how you do it."

Our fingers were still laced together, but it didn't feel strange to be holding hands with my team leader. Quite the opposite. It was as though by letting her in a little bit, her strength had called to mine. "Steps?" I asked.

A nod. "Tiny or big. Painful or not. Sometimes backward. Sometimes leaping across a gully in front of you. But then, one day, you'll look back, and you'll realize how far you've come, and . . . you'll be so damned proud of yourself."

Her voice broke, and I felt a tear slip down my cheek. "Not fair, Hannah."

She swiped at her own eye with a finger. "I'm a regular fucking philosopher, aren't I?"

I chuckled, glanced up at the ceiling while I got control of myself. "Why didn't I do this sooner?"

"Cry with me in your office?"

"Who's crying?"

We both glanced up, and I saw Lily in the open doorway. Her gaze flicked to our hands, still woven together. "Ah, come on," she grumbled, pushing into the office. "I'm getting jealous."

I laughed, even though it was watery. "You should be. I've decided that I'm going to start baring my soul at any number of uncomfortable moments."

She clapped her hands together, brown eyes mischievous, her long coffee-colored ponytail fluttering behind her shoulders like a horse's tail—an analogy I knew she wouldn't appreciate and thus, kept to myself.

"Oh," she said, sitting on my desk on the opposite side of me. "I love uncomfortable sharing. Should we talk about the time that my mom came into my room with breakfast and balloons the morning after I lost my virginity?"

My brows lifted, a chuckle bursting free.

Hannah shook her head, slipped her hand free. "She didn't."

Lily's brows rose. "You've met my mom. What do you think?"

Hannah started laughing. "I think she doesn't play."

"No," Lily said, "she doesn't. My girlfriend and I were both naked, and I was worrying about waking her up and telling her how to sneak her out of the house when my mom just came in with a breakfast tray with two plates."

Giggles burst out of me, quite painful with my stitches.

"She *didn't*," Hannah exclaimed again.

"Oh, she did," Lily told us. "Along with congratulatory balloons." She shook her head. "And her Polaroid camera. She snapped a picture, and it's in my baby book."

"A picture of you losing your virginity is in your baby book?"

My stomach ached from holding back a roar of laughter.

"Well, it's more of a milestone book, since she kept it going until I was twenty-five." Lily shrugged. "First steps. First period. First fucking."

I glanced at Hannah. She was biting her lip, eyes dancing.

And then we both lost it, roaring with laughter, Lily joining in, until eventually, we managed to control ourselves.

"Needless to say, my girlfriend decided that she couldn't put up with celebratory balloons and morning-after pictures. We broke up not long after that." Her tone was light. "But I got what I wanted, which was just as well."

I swiped my eyes, wiping the tears away. Twice in the span of ten minutes, and yet for completely different reasons.

Reasons I wouldn't trade for the world.

"What did you get?" Hannah asked.

Lily waggled her brows. "Orgasms."

I froze again.

"Admit it," she said. "It's the best thing I could have wanted."

My lips twitched. Hannah coughed.

Then we all dissolved into laughter once more.

———

"I'M LETTING LEO GO."

We were sitting on my bed, empty plates around us, the remains of our dinner—chicken, rice, salads, and more chocolate cake (because KTS agents have major sweet tooths), and we were—not really—watching a terrible horror movie on TV.

After the fifth or sixth time someone was eaten by a sand shark (yes, really), I'd lost interest and focused on my cake.

But now my fork had scraped empty ceramic and . . . I wanted this off my chest.

Lily lifted her brows, and I realized what that sounded like.

"We never did anything. I just—" I sighed. "I'm letting my fantasy of him go." I nibbled at my bottom lip, everything inside me telling me to keep this truth close to my chest, that

Hannah and Lily had already sent plenty of pity in my direction over Leo, and I didn't need to give them more ammunition for it. But . . . I'd been holding things close for so long and . . . I was tired.

So damned tired.

And it felt good to share.

Why couldn't this be something more? Why couldn't *I* be something more? There wasn't *any* reason, sad as it was, to be just discovering that now.

"I dreamed about him one day seeing me and sweeping me off my feet or falling madly in love or . . . I don't know, deciding that he wanted me and seeing the person I was hiding beneath. But he doesn't see me that way, so I'm letting it go." A sigh. "Letting the fantasies go. *All* of them. Him. Mine. I want to build something that's real, with people who see me as . . ."

I trailed off, my new leaf turned over, but my journey not complete, not yet anyway.

It wasn't easy to cut through twenty-plus years of blaming myself for everything that was wrong in my life, everything that had ever gone wrong.

A squeeze to my hand drew me out, and I stared up into Lily's gaze, her eyes serious for once. "You want people who see the wonderful, talented woman you are."

Genuine words.

Warmth in her deep brown eyes.

Yet my first instinct was to deny the compliment, to self-deprecate. Today, however, I laid that particular burden to rest and simply said, "Thank you."

Lily smiled approvingly.

"Do you know why I recruited you to my team?" Hannah asked into the silence that fell.

Surprise had me glancing over at her, my mouth dropping open. "No."

"Or why Landon was furious when I poached you from right beneath his nose?"

I shook my head.

"It's because the only one who doesn't see your worth is you."

My eyes flew to Lily, who nodded.

My lungs froze, a sharp inhale caught halfway between my nose and throat. Then I released it slowly, my words slipping out despite myself. "And Leo," I whispered. "He didn't see it."

"Oh, no." Hannah shook her head. "Leo's problem is that he saw it."

"What?" My brows drew together. That didn't make sense.

"He saw how bright you burn beneath that quiet exterior, and he couldn't look away. Like his retina were singed from staring at the sun, and then everything else in his life, including himself, were far too dark to ever dare to be close to you." Hannah squeezed my hand one more time and then released it. "He wants you—anyone could see that. His problem is that *he* thinks he's far too dark, and he can't bring the shadows close, for fear of disrupting the way you shine."

"I—"

That didn't make sense.

None of it made sense.

No one wanted me to be part of anything, least of all saw me as someone as great, as gorgeous as Leo. I was just a grunt who knew how to dismantle explosives. If someone wanted fodder to protect the rest of the agency, then I would be there.

Bomb fuel.

That was it. That was all—

No.

Just . . . *no.*

Because even on the most dangerous of missions, even when I'd been concerned about my abilities to get the job done, to render the explosive inert and had urged my teammates to leave, they'd stayed. My former team—Landon and Leo, Brett, Raj, and Mica. My current one. They hadn't left me behind, even though I was determined to remain.

I was part of something, despite doing my level best to avoid it.

"Just keep taking those steps, okay?" Hannah said. "Keep thinking. Keep with that epiphany and hold tight to that strength and courage. The rest of the pieces will fall into place."

Pieces falling in place. How did Hannah know this shit?

Lily asked the question for me. "How do you know that?"

Hannah grinned at both of us. "Call it intuition. Or stubborn team leader-ness." A laugh. "And also, maybe because now that we both know you feel this way, we won't let you slide back into your shell."

Lily high-fived her.

I inhaled.

"Don't overthink it," Hannah said.

I glared. "You just told me to *keep* thinking."

"Do one." A shrug. "Or the other." Another. "Either way, it'll work out." She stood, started collecting plates.

"That's not helpful!" I called.

"Now you know the other side of friendship."

I frowned.

"That I can be really annoying."

"I knew that before."

Lily pouted. "You took my line!"

Hannah chuckled. "Damn, and here I thought I had you fooled, as well."

I threw a balled-up napkin at her . . . which she easily dodged. "You're not funny."

A wink. "And yet, you're my friend anyway."

"Not for long," I called.

"Lies," she set the plates on the tray we'd had delivered then disappeared into the bathroom. I was still glaring at the empty hall when she popped her head back in, eyes sparkling with humor. "Oh, and by the way, this is your friend telling you to get some rest."

I wrinkled my nose. "I'm—"

Lily stood, asked innocently. "Going to listen to my friend so our team leader doesn't make it an order?"

Hannah nodded. "What she said."

I sighed. "Not even five minutes after our heart-to-heart, and you're already pulling the team leader card?"

"Damn right, I am."

Then Hannah surprised me by crossing over to my bed and grabbing me into a tight hug. My stitches pulled, and I smothered a wince, but I hugged her back, soaked in her whispered, "You're bright and beautiful, and I'm lucky to have a friend like you." She pulled back slightly. "Now, don't be a stubborn ass next time, okay?"

I laughed. "No guarantees."

"That's my girl," Lily said, nudging between us to give me a hug that was far gentler. She turned to Hannah. "Come on, I'll walk you back to your room."

Hannah lifted a brow. "Don't trust me?"

"Don't make me pull my second-in-command-ness," Lily said. "You need sleep, just as much as the rest of us."

Hannah laughed. "Hell, no, I don't."

Lily rolled her eyes but deliberately threaded her arm through Hannah's and tugged her from my room. "See you in the morning, Jesse-bug."

"Jesse-bug?" I asked archly.

A grin. "Okay, it's not the perfect nickname, but I'll work on it."

"*We* will work on it," Hannah said.

The door opened and closed, and I reclined on the bed, blinking after the hurricane of the last hour.

And thinking that *we* sounded perfect.

CHAPTER NINETEEN

Leo

I was waiting outside Hannah's quarters.

Had been waiting, for almost two hours now.

She hadn't been in her office, or Lily's, or Linc's, or Jesse's. She wasn't in the cafeteria or the pool or the shooting range. She almost seemed like she was avoiding me, except . . . *why* would she be avoiding me?

She didn't know Jess had asked me to leave.

She didn't know I was going to.

Right after we figured out who'd shot her.

So I waited, propped against the wall next to Hannah's room as the hours passed, trying to formulate some sort of plan to track down the traitors in our midst, yet also knowing I had nothing that no one else hadn't already thought of. I only managed to grow my frustration. It whipped through me, barbed and slicing, and making it nearly impossible for me to breathe.

I'd nearly lost her. No, I *had* lost her.

And I was the asshole who hadn't realized what I'd had until I'd lost it.

Not true. Well, not *entirely* true, because I was only just starting to recognize that I'd shoved Jesse so firmly into a box, into friendship because some part of me understood that just peeking beneath the lid would be a Pandora's box of emotions that I couldn't allow to grow.

Just thinking about having her in my life that way made terror rip through me, even more powerful than the pain of never seeing her again.

"At least if I don't see her, she'll be safe."

"Are you sure about that?"

My head jerked up from where I'd been studying the artistic qualities of my shoelaces to see Hannah in front of me. Lily slanted a glance in my direction before disappearing down the hall and into her quarters.

Some secret agent, huh?

I hadn't even heard them approach.

"I'm leaving."

A blond brow arched. "What are you doing, Leo?"

I didn't know. I didn't *fucking* know.

My chin dropped to my chest, and I went back to studying my laces. "She wants me to leave, so I'm going."

"She *wants* you," Hannah murmured. "Has wanted you for years."

I shook my head. "No. I ruined that, and even if I didn't, Jess and I couldn't ever—"

"Because she's not pretty enough for you?"

My anger flashed, and I had her pinned between my body and the wall before I even realized I'd moved. "She is the most beautiful woman I've ever seen." And she was. Maybe I hadn't recognized that before, maybe I'd been too much of a fucking ostrich to acknowledge it and what my draw to her might mean, had known it was safer if she were my friend and nothing more. And maybe someone else wouldn't see what I did, but when I looked at Jesse, I thought of moonlight and silver skin, of freckles and a sweet smile, of a strong, smart, kind woman who was burrowed deep into my heart.

Why had I ever thought it would be safe with just friendship?

I was so fucked.

I pressed harder. "Anyone who says differently will have to answer to me."

"Easy, dumbass," Hannah said with a smirk, her hand coming to my wrist, her thumb digging into a pressure point that made fingers I hadn't even realized were clenched on her neck spasm open to release her.

A flash of movement, aided by my shame at hurting another teammate, and I was the one slammed against the concrete wall.

"Too bad I'm not straight," she muttered. "What with those flashing green eyes and those *lips*, you'd"—she released me, chef-kissed—"be a treat."

I rolled my eyes, gritted. "I know I'm not your type."

She smiled, her eyes dancing. "Doesn't mean I can't appreciate pretty."

Fury was tearing through me, weaving with fear and hurt and inevitably. None of this would make any difference. I turned away, inhaled, exhaled slowly. "I'm going to find out who hurt her."

The amusement left her voice. "And then you're leaving?"

My throat was tight, so I just nodded, gaze on the opposite wall.

She grabbed my shoulder, spun me to face her, jaw clenched. "Seriously?"

"It's *all* she's asked of me," I said, jerking out from beneath her hand. "It's all I can give her."

"Bullshit." A sharp slap of a curse.

"I'm leaving," I repeated.

"So, you're just going to give up?" she asked, tossing her hands up, her rage a mirror of mine. "You're not even going to try? You're in love with that woman, and you're just going to *walk away?*"

I balled my hands into fists, a heartbeat away from slamming them into the wall. "What the fuck am I supposed to do? I can't be with her, not like she deserves."

"Why?"

As if that were an easy question to answer, as if it wouldn't reveal every dark and pitiful and shameful thing inside me. Just *why?* Bile rose, burned the back of my throat. I gave in to the urge, slammed my fist into the wall, felt the skin over my knuckles break open, and because that pain felt so good, I kept punching, over and over and over—

Hannah gripped my arm, yanked it away from the concrete, her nails biting into my flesh.

"You fight for her," she said.

A simple statement.

I shook my head, skittered back like a fucking coward.

I *couldn't* fight for her. Not when it might mean—

Hannah moved with me, clenching tighter until I felt her nails puncture my skin, blood oozing down my arm. "Jesse deserves to have someone fight for her," she snapped. "She *deserves* to be with someone who'll rip off every barrier and be vulnerable, who will protect her, to show her that she matters when she questions that herself." Hannah released me, shoved me back a step. "Be that man, Leo," she whispered.

"I can't—" I bit my tongue until I felt it bleed. "I just . . . can't."

Hannah's hazel eyes were filled with disappointment, with disgust. But she couldn't look at me with any more repulsion than I already felt. It was soldered into my bones, clung to the DNA in my every cell.

"Then heaven help you when Jesse finds that man who will."

She placed her palm on her lock, pushed open the door to her quarters.

"Because she will," Hannah said. "And it won't take long."

CHAPTER TWENTY

Jesse

A WEEK LATER, I was sitting across the table from a man I didn't want to look at.

A man who'd hurt me.

A man who I'd allowed to hurt me.

And I was struggling with distance, to hold on to the fury that had finally pushed me to declare it was just enough.

Because of the shadows in his eyes.

Haunted.

He was . . . broken, changed, altered, and he wasn't hiding the fact. It was written all over his face, and I hated that I was the one who'd done that. Was it truly his fault that I'd loved him and hadn't done shit about it? Of course not. Did he deserve my censure just because he'd never looked at me the same way I had him? Yes, it was true he'd hurt my feelings, had been a bit of a jerk. No, he'd been a raging asshole.

But he'd been my friend before that.

So . . . guilt.

Even though I was telling myself—my new and improved, no longer hiding self—that it wasn't my fault.

Leo had been a jerk. He deserved it.

And I'd—God, why couldn't I just lie to myself? It would be so much easier than feeling guilty, especially when I'd spent the last week trying to convince myself that I had absolutely nothing to feel guilty about.

I wasn't the one who'd been an asshole.

I wasn't the one who'd looked at me in disgust, who'd revolted at my touch.

I was just the one who'd created a shit-ton of expectations and fantasies, and even while telling myself they could never come true, I'd still hoped that maybe . . . he might see me as someone who he could want.

It wasn't his fault that I wasn't what he wanted.

Even despite Hannah's talk of bright and shadows, and her being convinced his lack of interest in me wasn't because he didn't feel anything, but rather because he couldn't allow himself to *feel* anything. That was fantasy, and I couldn't allow myself to go back there.

But . . . I could be a nice person.

I didn't have to make myself small to show him kindness, especially when he was clearly feeling guilty about hurting me.

I cleared my throat, felt his gaze come to my face, though I deliberately kept mine directed toward the window until I could speak with an even tone. "Where's everyone else?" I asked, meeting his eyes.

He shrugged. "Not sure."

And we went back to silence, waiting for a meeting that was supposed to start ten minutes ago, waiting for Linc, Lily, and Hannah to walk through the door. Supposedly, they had intel we needed to see and a mission in the imminent future.

I waited another five minutes before I pulled my phone out and sent Hannah a text.

Then waited another five—with no response—before texting Linc and Lily.

Was cell service down?

No, I had four bars, not to mention we had a satellite backup, thanks to a mission gone wrong with Dan and Ava, where their phones hadn't worked. We were supposed to be able to reach each other under any circumstance.

Which meant—

I dropped my cell on the table, lurched up out of my seat.

"What?"

I strode to the door, yanked on the handle.

Locked.

Leo was at my side in an instant, spice and male surrounding me. "What is it?" he asked, and I realized the shadows under his eyes were even darker up close. I wanted to stroke my finger across them, as though I could wipe the small bruises away, as though I could take his hurt.

Take *his* hurt?

Why would I do that?

I heard Hannah's voice in my head, *Because you're a good fucking person?*

I was. I could think that with confidence now—progress made. But I still wasn't going to do it. Instead, I moved back to the table, picked up my cell, and called Hannah.

Nothing.

Then Lily. Also nothing.

Then Linc and Olive and Ava and Dan and Laila and Ryker.

Conveniently, none of them were available to take my call. Frustrated that they were pushing this, that they were forcing me to take a step with Leo I didn't feel ready for—absolution? resolution? closure?—I stomped around the table and picked up Leo's phone, repeating the process with calls.

All to no answer.

What did they think would happen? A locked door and some forced proximity would resolve everything, and we'd fall in love, happily ever after?

I'd just stopped kidding myself.

I didn't need to hop back aboard the fantasy train.

Leo's cell buzzed, and I glanced down at the screen, saw it was a text from me.

I'm sorry.

I glanced up, saw he held my phone, and sighed, wanting to tell him his apology didn't make one bit of difference.

Except, it kind of did.

My fingers moved on the screen, and I sent a reply.

I'm sorry, too.

He froze when my cell buzzed then glanced down at the screen, and I saw everything inside him relax as he read the simple message.

"But we're still trapped," I said, "and unless you're about to go Hulk on the door"—because only a superhero would be able to bust through the thick concrete-based doors and reinforced hinges—"we're stuck here until Hannah and company decide to let us out."

His eyes went surprised. "You think they locked us in here?"

"You think for a second they didn't?" I asked, rolling my eyes. "They were done with us fighting and wanted us to talk."

A beat of quiet, then, "Well, I guess it worked." He crossed over to me, my phone still gripped in his hand, his in mine. "Are you okay?"

I was more okay than I'd been in a long time.

But all I said was, "I'm getting there."

Deep green eyes holding mine, searching, peering down into the depths of my soul. He'd never looked at me like that before, and my heart beat faster, my throat went dry. Want. It was there in his gaze.

Except, he *didn't* want.

I turned away, strode to the windows, stared out through the tinted glass, watching the common area. The sun was going down, so the space wasn't full, just a few stragglers walking across the grass, probably on their way to dinner.

"Did you come up with a name for your owl, yet?"

I hadn't, so I just shook my head.

Quiet, but I sensed him drawing nearer. My nape prickled with awareness, the scar on my thigh throbbed.

His thumb brushed over the bullet wound on the back of my neck, and I had to lock my knees against them buckling. God, I hoped I'd find another man whose touch made my bones feel like they would melt. "I'm sorry about this, too."

I frowned, spun. "That wasn't your fault."

His eyes told me he didn't believe me. His words confirmed it. "You nearly died saving me."

"It's my job to have your back," I said, echoing his words from that night.

"I don't like seeing you hurt. Whether it's from a bullet or from me."

"I know." I finally gave in and brushed one dark circle then the other.

"I'm sorry."

A laugh slid out of me. "You said that already."

"This wasn't about that night or the days before. This was"—his eyes were pained—"for all the rest of it."

An apology for me falling in love with him. Because he thought he didn't deserve it? Because I wasn't the only one with self-worth issues? Because we'd both made mistakes and missed—

Our bodies drifted together. His fingers skated across my cheek, gently tucked a lock of my hair behind my ear. Our lips were nearly touching, and I could feel his breath on my skin.

And . . . I gave in.

I pressed my mouth to his.

Electric.

Sparks shivered down my spine, my nerves exploded with sensation. His tongue trailed across my bottom lip, daring me to open, and I did, was rewarded when it slid into my mouth, danced alongside mine, those sparks turning into fire, coalescing into a moan that drifted from my mouth to his.

A moan that made him freeze.

That had him pulling back, his fingers thrusting deeply into his hair and gripping tight. "I can't do this," he said, soft and tortured. Then he was across the room, his fist colliding with the door, as though he were taking my earlier joke about Hulk seriously and was going to bust his way out of here. "I *can't* do this."

"Because I'm me?" I asked, the question slipping out, even though it went against every bit of the last week, of my new leaf, of those pieces slipping back into place.

The words floated across the room with almost palpable weight, and when they hit Leo's ears, the reaction was instantaneous. He went ramrod stiff, spun away from the door, and was in front of me in a second. "God no, Jesse," he said hoarsely, his hands on my cheeks. "This isn't—" He broke off, released me with a tortured shake of his head, spinning away, his chest rising and falling like he'd run a marathon.

"It's not you. It's me. It's—"

Pain in those rasped-out sentences.

Pain that called to the pain inside me.

I gently placed my hand on his shoulder. "I understand," I said, squeezing lightly. "It's okay. You don't have to say anything."

Then I released him and went back to the window.

A weight had disappeared from my chest. Not me. *Not* me. Hannah had been right. Whatever Leo had going on wasn't on me.

And for right now, that was enough.

Because it gave me hope that maybe, one day, we might find our way back to being friends.

CHAPTER TWENTY-ONE

Leo

I DIDN'T EVEN REALIZE I still held the cell phone in one hand until it buzzed.

Fight for her.

"It's not that fucking easy, Hannah!" I wanted to roar up at the ceiling, my eyes going to the camera in the corner of the room, as I glared into the black lens.

Another buzz.

I'm turning it off.

My fingers tapped across the screen.

Unlock the fucking door.

Nothing. Then,

Fight, Leo. For her. For you.

If it was my cell, I would have launched it across the room, would have stomped on the pieces with pleasure. But it was Jesse's phone, and I didn't want to hurt her, even by ruining her electronics.

I'd done more than enough of that already.

So, I carefully set it on the table and moved to one of the chairs, sinking into it and knowing they couldn't keep us here forever.

At some point, they'd need to feed and water us, at least.

Or take us to the bathroom.

Another buzz.

There's a portable toilet in the corner and MREs in the cabinet.

I glared at the camera.

I promise, it's going off now.

The phone didn't buzz again, and I sighed, my gaze glued to Jesse's back as she stared off into the yard. Probably, looking for her owl.

"You should name her Luna."

Jesse's shoulders stiffened, and she spun around. "What are you talking about?"

"Your owl."

She frowned.

"I saw you in the moonlight, and it changed my life."

Shit. I shouldn't have said that. I opened my mouth to add something else, to take it back, to step behind that barrier in my mind and heart . . . and I found I couldn't. Just as I couldn't stop the words from pouring out. "You were beautiful," I murmured. "You *are* beautiful. So much so that it takes my breath away, makes me crazy to know that there are people out there who hurt you, who left marks on that beautiful skin." My fingers clenched on the arms of my chair.

"Leo," she whispered.

I didn't dare look at her.

"Yeah, I wanted you to be my friend," I said, still looking down. "I didn't want that to change because I know that I can't give you more. I'm not the type of man—" I broke off before I could say more, could say something that might make this about me.

All of a sudden, my chair was shoved back, and Jesse was in front of me.

"What?" she snapped. "You're not the type of man who what?"

I was frozen in place, couldn't dare lift a finger, not when her hands rested on my knees, all but pinning me in place with the barest amount of pressure.

"Answer me," she snapped. "You're not the kind of man who what?"

She was so close, and my hands itched to tug her into my lap.

"The type of man who likes a woman like me?" Her brows rose. "The type of man who only likes tiny, curvy little women who are easy to toss around and dominate?"

"What? *No!*" I exclaimed.

Her body—fuck it, was all I dreamed about. I'd tasted her skin. Once. And the silken, sweet taste was imprinted on my soul.

"Then what? You're not the type of man who likes a woman who can beat him in an accuracy contest?"

My fingers clenched tighter. The arms of the chair groaned in protest. "*No.*"

"Then why, Leo? I've spent so fucking much of my life thinking I'm not the type of woman who a man like you could love. That I'm too muscular. That my hair is too red. That I'm too quiet. That—"

"You're *none* of those things," I snapped. "None of this is on you. I've wanted you for a long time, even when I pretended I didn't."

"Why pretend?" Her hands tightened on my knees. "If you wanted me, why would you pretend?"

Something snapped.

I erupted to my feet, grabbing her by the waist and plunking her on the edge of the table, staring into those gorgeous blue eyes, tracking the freckles, the flush trailing across her cheeks. "Because I'm not good enough for you!" I yelled.

"Bullshit!" she yelled back. "I spent my whole life thinking I wasn't good enough for anyone, that I was fucking worthless, and I'm done with that. Done with other people doing that. Done with *you* doing that." Her voice softened. "I know you, Leo. I know what kind of man you are, and it's a good one. Why do you think I fell in love with you? Why do you think I dreamed about you for so long?"

Her mouth was right there. I could smell her shampoo, could see the freckle on her lip I'd fantasized tracing with my tongue more times than I could count. It would be so easy to take her, to kiss her, to—

"You wouldn't have dreamed if you knew."

Her fingers clenched on my shoulders. "Knew *what?*"

"That I'll end up killing you."

I dropped my hands, spun away from her, and moved to the camera. "Let me the fuck out of here, or I'm taking a chair to the window."

Silence.

Jesse's phone buzzed.

Then a soft hand dropped onto my back. "It wouldn't work," Jess whispered. "The glass is bomb proof."

The hand left, and I felt a part of myself leave with her.

It was over.

Done.

The truth was out, and—

Screech.

Blinking, I turned in time to see Jess pushing one of the large side cabinets toward the corner with the camera, the pitcher of water sitting on top of it shaking as it moved, liquid sloshing over the top. Before I could grab it, before I could say anything, before I could react other than standing there like a wide-eyed dumbass, she climbed on top, reached for the camera, and yanked it out of the wall.

"There," she said, calm as can be, tossing it into a nearby trash can before hopping down and wiping her hands together. "Now, tell me what the hell you're talking about."

I glanced from her to my own hands, half expecting them to be covered with her blood, with Clem's blood.

But they were there, unstained, faint scars on the fingers and backs.

Hands that had held another woman I'd considered dear.

Hands that had killed her.

Hands that were then covered by Jesse's.

I went to snatch them away, unable to see beyond the past and all the things that had happened with Clem, but Jess gripped me tighter, and the only thing my jerking accomplished was to bring her body flush against me.

Flowers in my nose. Curves pressed to my chest.

Eyes staring deeply into mine.

"Leo," she said, and the gentle in her tone was what got me.

My knees buckled, and I ripped my hands from hers. That night, God, that night, it was washing over me again, and I couldn't take it, not with Jess so close, not with the memories so vast.

She sank down with me, crawling into my lap and holding me tight.

"It's okay," she whispered, "it's okay. I'm sorry. You don't have to tell me anything."

I realized I was crying, tears dripping down my cheeks. I hadn't cried that night. I'd been too numb to do anything more than to stare blankly at my hands, at the blood, knowing that

I'd killed Clem, that it was my fault. And I hadn't cried since, not as the guilt had swallowed me up, and I'd let it keep me beneath the surface.

Not as I'd lost myself in work.

Not as the years had gone by, and I'd been careful to not care.

Drowning in grief until Jess had joined my team in London. Bright red hair, big blue eyes, quiet—so damned quiet that I'd surfaced, had wanted to hear her, wanted to make her smile.

Just as friends.

I'd held tight to that notion because I was really fucking good at pretending.

Her hands came to my cheeks, her thumbs brushing away the tears before she wrapped her arms around me and held me tightly. "I'm sorry," she murmured. "I'm so sorry."

My ear rested against her chest, and I could hear her heart pounding against her ribs, feel her pulse skittering against my skin.

A drop of liquid plunked onto my head, and then another and another, until I realized that Jess was crying.

And that—her pain—finally snapped me out of it.

I shifted, taking her into *my* arms, crushing her against my chest. "Don't apologize," I said. "It's me. It's me. Please, don't cry."

She sniffed, rubbed her face against my chest, and went still.

Both of us were breathing heavily, and I knew I was holding her too tight, knew I should release her.

But my hands didn't work.

Instead, my voice did.

"I was married," I whispered. "Young and stupid, and I fell in love with a girl named Clementine." Jess shifted, sitting up enough to meet my eyes, and I saw they were so damned gentle. "Clem was a redhead." I ran my fingers through Jesse's hair, tugged lightly on one strand. "With green eyes to match mine and a temper that was off the charts."

She smiled gently.

"We weren't peaceful or calm. We fought *all* the time. Broke up more often than we were together." I shook my head. "But we loved each other. For better or worse, we loved each other."

Jess waited, but the questions were there in her blue eyes, even as I struggled to put everything into words.

"It was getting to a point where things were going to end. I was at work all the time, KTS had recruited me, and I was seriously considering accepting the position. But they needed me in London, and Clem didn't want to leave her job." I shook my head. "I was a mess. We'd gotten married too young and changed too much."

"That happens," Jess murmured when I fell quiet again.

"Yes," I said, "it does."

Her hands were on my shoulders, and she squeezed lightly. "What happened, baby?"

I inhaled sharply. "We fought that night, one of the biggest we'd ever had. We both said some stuff that was . . . shitty. Really fucking shitty." A sigh. "We were immature and lashing out, and she screamed that she was going to leave me."

And this was the part that I couldn't get over.

Jesse's fingers tightened.

"And I told her to go. Despite the fact that she'd been drinking, I told her to get the fuck out. I let her take her keys, her car, allowed her to drive away." My eyes closed, my voice going hoarse. "By the time I realized what was happening and followed, it was too late."

I saw the scene like it was right in front of me.

"We lived on a winding road. It was dark and raining, and I turned the corner."

Jess was so, *so* still in my arms.

Still, like Clem had been.

"She'd slid off the road, and she hadn't been wearing her seat belt."

"Leo," Jess breathed.

"I found her in the road." I met Jesse's stare. "I couldn't save her. She was . . . gone." Blood on my hands. Her body so still, so lifeless in my arms. "I hurt her. I let her go, and she died."

"But you didn't kill her."

My jaw clenched. Logically, I knew she was right. But I might as well have driven the car off the road myself. Might as well have unbuckled her seat belt. Poured that wine down her throat.

"Leo, it wasn't your fault."

I jumped to my feet, sending Jess tumbling out of my arms, and before I could steady her, she'd found her own stability, her own feet next to me. "Then whose fucking fault was it?"

"No one's," she said. "It was a horrible accident."

That wasn't good enough.

Not for me. Not for her.

I'd already hurt Jess, nearly gotten her killed on a mission. Yes, I wanted her. But, no, I couldn't have her, not when I might be responsible for her getting hurt or dying. God, look what I'd already done.

"And let me guess," she said, and I blinked at the cold tone of her voice. "You're going to hold on to that guilt, wrap it like a blanket around you, and you don't even give a shit about what I want."

"You told me to go."

"Yes," she said, stepping back and crossing her arms.

Ask me to stay.

Please, fucking *please* ask me to stay.

"I did. I told you to go." Her arms dropped. "And I'm not going to ask you to stay."

CHAPTER TWENTY-TWO

Jesse

I WATCHED HIS FACE FALL, and I hated that I'd caused it.

But I meant what I said.

I wasn't going to beg him to stay for me. I needed him to *want* to do that for me, to fight for me, to show me that I was worth the battle, the pain, letting go of the guilt and fear.

He turned away, thrust his hands into his hair.

"I can't fight your guilt *and* my own," I whispered. "I can't bolster my self-worth *and* yours. I can only be me, trying to move beyond my past, and hoping that you'll be able to move beyond yours."

He spun back, agony in those green eyes, and I knew he was where I'd spent the last years—firmly in the grip of the past.

Only Leo could pull himself out.

But perhaps, I could give him a shove.

"Do you know what I thought when I first met you?"

Mutely, he shook his head.

"I thought a man as gorgeous as you would never, *ever* look twice at a woman like me. Because I thought you had all the value, and I had none." My voice dipped. "I didn't think I was worth a second look, let alone someone understanding that I was a woman with real worth."

He closed the distance between us, gripped my shoulders. "That's bullshit. You're worth so much, Jess. You're beautiful, and I don't just mean the package on the outside. I've dreamed about you since that night in the moonlight, dreamed of kissing every freckle on your nose and cheeks. I've thought about trailing my tongue along your beautiful throat. I've been desperate to be between your gorgeous thighs."

My hands shook, and I lifted them to loosen his hold on my shoulders, his grip growing painfully hard.

He gentled, but his words came fast and furious. "I thought I could just be your friend," he said. "But then you left and came here, and I had this huge hole in my life. I knew it was better to leave you be, better to keep that hole empty—"

"Leo," I breathed, my heart hurting for him.

I knew that hole. I'd lived with that hole for too fucking long. I didn't want that for this man—who'd been kind to me when I'd first joined KTS, who'd been my support and a good friend when I was feeling out of my depth, who'd come here and fought against the same connection I'd fantasized about and run from in equal measures.

"I couldn't stay away. I applied for the open position as soon as I saw it, kidding myself that it was only because I wanted to find the traitors."

He didn't want to find the traitors? I frowned, opened my mouth.

"I want to find them," he said. "I want to wipe them off the fucking planet, but that wasn't the real reason I came."

My heart was pounding now.

"I came for you." His hands cupped my cheeks. "Even when I didn't understand what was in my heart and head, I came for you."

I leaned in, needing to hold him, needing to kiss and touch and stroke him.

But then he dropped his hands and turned away. "But it doesn't change anything."

It took me a minute because I couldn't believe what the fuck he was saying. Leo had just told me all of those beautiful things, and he was still going to walk away? My words stoppered up in my throat, and I stood there frozen for a long moment.

Then I boiled over.

The kind, understanding, sweet Jess left the fucking building and I'd. Had. Enough.

I'd come this far. He'd shared what he had.

And *still* he was going to walk away?

Fuck that.

"You fucking bastard," I snapped. Spinning toward him, I gripped his arms and swept my leg between his, knocking him off balance and shoving him back. We collapsed into a heap that took my breath for several heartbeats. Then I was slamming my fists against his chest. "Fuck you. Fuck you for saying that. Fuck you for not fighting for me. Fuck—"

He grabbed my wrists, held them fast, trapping them against him.

"You!" I yelled.

His eyes flared, heat and anger in the depths, and one abrupt movement had me on my back, Leo on top of me, all the heavy lines of his muscled body pressing into mine.

"I know, baby," he murmured. "I'm sorry."

My lungs were heaving, my wrists still held in his hands, and I shifted, breaking the grip, digging my nails into his chest. "No," I growled. "You don't get to be sorry, not when you won't take a fucking chance and be with me."

"Sweetheart," he moaned, resting his forehead against mine. "I can't."

"You won't."

"I—"

I wrapped my hands around his waist, bringing him flush

against me, feeling the hard length of his erection, the heavy weight of his hips.

His breathing accelerated, hot puffs on my lips.

His eyes were on fire, burning up for me.

"You won't," I breathed.

"I—"

"Can," I finished.

His breath shuddered out, scattering over my throat, making me shiver, and I don't know if I moved or if he did, but suddenly—*finally*—we were kissing.

And it was everything I had ever dreamed.

His tongue slid across my lips, dipped into my mouth as he angled my head so that our kiss drew deeper. Heat was flaring in my abdomen, shooting out through my veins, making my fingers tingle, my pussy ache. Everything was burning up from my toes to my breasts. Even my hair felt like it was on fire.

I clenched my legs tighter, bucked against his cock, and his groan tumbled from his mouth to mine.

Then his lips were trailing over my chin, my jaw, down my throat.

"You smell so fucking good, Jess," he rasped, releasing my hands to tug the neck of my shirt to the side, his teeth grazing my collarbone.

I couldn't reply, not when he was touching me like this, when his body was poised over mine, when his lips were on my skin. I couldn't do anything other than to moan and use my newly freed hands to pull him closer.

But he merely reared back, out of my hold.

The pang of disappointment sliced me to the quick.

Rip.

I gasped, blinking in shock when he tore my T-shirt straight down the front.

"Fuck," he hissed, and then he was on me again, only his lips bypassed mine, going straight to my newly exposed skin.

He yanked my bra up, pushed the halves of my T-shirt to the side, pinning my arms. "You are so fucking beautiful."

My heart skipped a beat, and I reached for him, wanting to touch him, only my arms were trapped in the material, my breasts out and on full display.

A fact he was very aware of.

His lips lowered and he sucked my nipple into his mouth.

"Shit," I breathed, arching up, trying to get him to suck me deeper, harder, even as sparks flew through me and my pussy was throbbing.

He switched sides.

I gasped, bucked, and managed to flip us, yanking my shirt off, tugging my bra over my head. I reached for the hem of his shirt, tugging it up, exposing the smooth planes of his stomach, the muscles of his abdomen etched and demanding my tongue. He shifted, trying to take it off, but I was too busy with the skin I'd revealed, too desperate to taste and touch him.

But then I was on my back again, and Leo was yanking at my jeans, flicking open the button, tugging the zipper down. They got stuck on my thighs, the pink scar standing out sharply in the fluorescent lights.

I froze, thinking it would bring everything back, that he would stop, and we'd be back to all of the pain and guilt from before.

Instead, he simply bent and kissed the line with such tenderness that I felt my eyes prickle. Then more than prickle when he rose and pressed his lips to the mark at the base of my throat.

"I'm sorry," he breathed against my skin.

My hands slid into his hair, and I tugged his head back. "No more," I whispered. "Please, no more."

Emerald eyes going sad, making my stomach sink.

But before I could delve into that feeling, determination slid into his expression, his hand coming up to cup my cheek. "No more," he breathed.

And he kissed me again.

It was soft and gentle, and those final tiny pieces that had been missing in my heart shifted, until there were no more holes.

"No more," he said again, kissing his way down my body, over my underwear, boring white cotton that he didn't seem to mind, based on the heated look he tossed my way, how he paused to suck my clit through the material.

My hips jerked, my fingers found his hair, trying to keep him there.

But he simply kept moving, sliding down my legs to where my jeans were bunched on my thighs, bypassing the tangled material and reaching for my boots. One was yanked off, tossed over his shoulder and landing somewhere behind us with a *thunk*. My other boot joined the first. Then my socks, with hardly any fanfare—or at least noise.

He rose back up over me, nudged the hem of my underwear to the side and licked me from top to bottom. I tried to spread my legs, but my jeans wouldn't let me, and he didn't seem to give a shit, just continued licking me.

My breath hissed out when his tongue touched a particularly sensitive spot.

"There, baby?" he asked, and him between my thighs, his lips glistening, my underwear still to the side. But that wasn't the sexiest thing. Nor were his strong arms clenching my hips, the stubble on his jaw. No, the absolute sexiest thing was the smile he gave me.

Arrogant, with plenty of erotic intent.

I was too blown away by that smile to answer his question, and anyway, Leo simply allowed that smile to grow into a smirk and sank back down, his hot words against my pussy. "Yeah, that's the spot." And then he stroked there again, making me jump, making me moan, making me forget all about the jeans keeping my legs trapped together. At least, until they were torn down my thighs, yanked over my feet, my underwear joining them in flying over his shoulder. He spread me wide, pressed his mouth to my pussy, and allowed his fingers to join the party, one thick digit shoving inside me, his lips going back to that spot, sucking deeply.

A shudder tore through me. "*Leo.*"

"No more," he whispered again, sliding another finger home, trailing his tongue over to my clit, flicking and stroking in a rhythm that showed me absolutely no mercy. "No more," he repeated, the words as much a caress as his tongue, as his fingers curling inside me.

He kept working me, not stopping when I continued to tremble, my head thrashing from side to side, my hips moving so I was all but fucking his face, his fingers as pleasure wound tight, expanded through my center.

I needed him, needed *more*, wanted him deep inside me, but when I begged him to, "get inside me," he simply laughed and shook his head. He slipped another finger into me, making me gasp and thrash against him. "Come, baby," he coaxed. "Come on my fingers, let me feel you clench around me."

"I can't," I moaned. It felt good, so fucking good, but I couldn't come, not without . . . "I need—*fuck!*" I screamed when he bit my clit, hard enough that pain and pleasure tangled together. It was too much and not enough and . . . then his tongue pressed firmly and—

I shattered.

My pleasure wasn't an explosion . . . it was a breaking and reforming. It was shards shooting in all directions, the blissful sensations so strong they almost hurt, and then it was as though time froze in place. For a moment. Only a moment. And then everything reversed and flew through the air, slamming back into me with enough force that every bit of my breath whooshed out of me.

I came to, tucked against Leo's side, his fingers brushing through my ponytail, moisture between my thighs, and his arms wrapped tight.

Pushing up, I stared into his eyes. "No more running from the past."

His lips went pale, but when he didn't back down, his hand lifting, his thumb running lightly over my jaw. "No more," he agreed.

I smiled. "I think that might be the favorite thing you've ever said to me."

A little humor entered his expression. "Wait until I say that about ice cream."

I groaned, swatted his chest. "For your sake, I hope you never do."

He trailed his hand down my throat, lightly brushed the scar from the bullet, dragged it over my shoulder, along my arm, over my hips. "For the record," he said, voice husky. "I don't want to talk about your body as being anything but the sexiest fucking thing I've ever laid eyes on ever again."

I snorted. "Leo."

His hand clamped down on my ass. "Never, baby." He held my stare, not looking away, not saying anything else until I nodded.

"No more," I said, taking a page out of his book, but then because I'd turned over my new leaf, because I was trying to be better, stronger, *more*, I cupped his cheeks (the ones on his face) and glared into his eyes. "So long as you promise that from this moment onward, we are going to look forward. No more past. No more regrets. I want my life to be *more*, and I want it to be with you."

Fear. Hope. Terror. Joy. They all flared across his face.

Maybe once that would have made me get smaller, to retreat.

But . . . *no more.*

"I can't promise not to get hurt," I said. "And the thought of you being injured on a mission scares the shit of out me."

He wrapped his arms around me, held me tight.

"But I want what we might have together more." I inhaled

his spicy scent, held him close. "I want it more than the fear, and I want it more than I want to hold on to the past."

"Jess," he said.

I leaned back. "So now, the only question here is, do you want that, too?"

Silence.

My heart squirmed in my chest, my intestines tied themselves into knots.

Then he smiled.

And I knew it would be okay.

CHAPTER TWENTY-THREE

Leo

I LOVED THIS WOMAN.

It was absolutely terrifying, and yet it was the one thing I was most certain of in all the world, and only second to that was that I wanted the possibility of us, too.

More than the fear.

More than the past.

More than continuing to punish myself for my part in it.

Jesse hadn't pulled away when I'd told her about Clem, hadn't looked at me with the disgust I felt for myself, and I felt as though some of the sharp shards inside me had been filed down, that they were no longer stabbing into my lungs. Finally, I could take a full breath. Finally, I felt as though the boulder on my shoulders had grown a little lighter.

"I want it," I said. "I want *you*."

Her blue eyes were bright with tears, and then she wrapped her arms around me and slanted her mouth over mine and kissed me.

Desire and need. My cock growing hard again in an instant,

pushing against the zipper of my jeans, desperate to be inside her. I still had her taste on my tongue. My fingers were still wet from being in her pussy.

But I wasn't going to fuck her on the floor of the conference room where anyone might walk in. I shouldn't have gotten her naked here, not when Hannah might get it in her mind to unlock that door at any moment and barge in here, slinging more orders around.

So, I broke away, hating that I had to lose her mouth, but knowing I needed to get her clothes.

Otherwise I *was* going to end up fucking her on the floor, or the table, or the wall . . . and none of those thoughts were helping me get my cock under control. And neither did Jess, not when she reached for me, groaning in protest.

It was fucking torture to capture her hands, to press a kiss to each palm, to slide away from her and retrieve her clothes.

"It's a goddamned crime against humanity that you have to wear clothes," I said, tugging her bra over her head.

She froze . . . and then laughed, shaking her head. "Oh, Leo," she moaned.

"Do that again when I'm inside you."

Her cheeks flushed pink, and it was more fucking torture to have to cover up her sexy body. But even so, I slipped my shirt over her head then returned for her jeans and socks, handing her the latter while I turned the former right side out. I was just reaching for her boots when she murmured, "I will."

Heat blazing down my spine.

Need exploding inside me.

I'd loosened the chokehold, had allowed myself to feel, and there was no going back.

I whipped around, saw that she was performing the sexiest little shimmy to wiggle into her jeans. "Promise you'll do *that* again with your tits out," I ordered, walking over to her and cupping her cheeks.

"I will," she murmured again.

"Fuck," I hissed.

Her brows rose. "You asked me to promise."

"And now, you're making me reconsider fucking you on the edge of the table."

"Fuck," she breathed, her body drifting close, pressing to mine. Her hand trailed down my chest, slid beneath the hem of my T-shirt. "Let's do *that*."

I groaned, picked her up, and slanted my mouth to hers, walking her to the table, plunking her on top of it, and stepping in between her thighs. Her tongue tangled with mine, her hands came to my ass, drawing me nearer. "Why did we wait so long to do this?" I asked, pulling back enough to allow her to breathe when she pushed at my chest.

Her lips curved. "I don't—"

I kissed her again, swallowing the rest of her statement, and gripped the rounded bevel of wood, hearing the table creak in protest.

That bolstered my control enough to retreat, my head hanging, resting on her shoulder, her hands gripping my hair tightly enough to sting before they slowly released, and I managed to step back from her. "You're dangerous."

A smile, sexy and confident, and I felt so damned lucky to have been given a glimpse of this woman.

I would never, fucking *never* do anything again that made her disappear.

And that promise was written in my soul.

I returned to her boots, helped her slip them on, tugging the laces so they were secure while she teased me and "my Cinderella vibes." Then I plunked myself onto the table next to her, tucking her hair behind her ears. "Any ideas how I can get out of here?"

Her cell buzzed, and she reached over to snag it, shaking her head at the screen.

She lifted it, showing me the message from Lily.

Safe word: Twinkle toes.

"I don't know what that means."

"Luckily, I do," Jess said, tapping the screen and putting it up to her ear. "Twinkle toes," she murmured.

The lock *clicked* on the door.

"Thank you," Jesse said, hanging up. She met my gaze and smirked. "Should we go?"

Love.

So much fucking love for this woman—almost too much, almost enough that it nearly had me running from the room, running for a plane back to London. But she had courage and strength, and she was looking at me in happiness and hope and joy and . . . I was damned if I was going to let her down.

"I'm going anywhere you want to, baby."

———

I'D INTENDED to take Jesse back to her room, to get her to groan my name while I was buried deep inside her, but work had other ideas.

"Thank God, you two sorted that," Lily said, striding up the moment we walked through the door and into the hall. Her brown hair was pulled back into a ponytail, and her gaze was serious. She tossed him a shirt. "Here you go, Romeo. Cover the abs. We've got a problem."

I was instantly on alert.

Jesse's fingers clenched in mine.

"Come on," Lily said. "We'll fill you in on the drive."

I met pale blue eyes, watched as Jesse hit the switch in her mind from woman to KTS agent, knew that I needed to do that same, but it was a struggle. Not just because of the desire to claim her in every way, but because I had no doubt that we were about to go into danger.

And I might not be able to protect her.

Another squeeze of her fingers and I shoved that down as we followed Lily to the locker room, joining Linc and Hannah as all of us efficiently geared up.

"Here's the situation," she said, velcroing on a bulletproof vest. "Laila and her team had a bead on Daniel. They went in to recon, and it's turned into a firefight. We're getting on a chopper, and we're going to get them out."

I shoved my gun into its holster, made sure I had extra magazines, knew my teammates were all doing the same, knew Jess was doing it.

Hannah gave more instructions, and I dutifully filed them away, even as fear crawled up my throat.

I felt so much more for Jess than I'd *ever* felt for Clem.

It was fucking terrifying, petrifying.

But I pushed it down.

I needed to focus if I was going to keep her safe, needed to focus if I was going to keep *all* of my teammates safe.

We finished gearing up, sprinted out to the parking garage and up to the roof to the helipad. Wind whipped over my face from the chopper's blades, and we all instinctively ducked as we ran and jumped onto the helicopter, buckled in, and threw on our headsets as we took off.

"Fifteen minutes out," Hannah said through the mic, holding up an iPad with a map displayed on its screen. "We'll drop in here," she said, pointing to a spot on the map. "Laila and team are bogged down here. More support is coming from here"—she zoomed out enough to show the road that led into the compound—"and here"—another road on the south side of the property—"We're going to haul ass, get in there, provide backup and evaluate, and then we're going to sit tight until the rest of the teams get here."

"How long?" Jesse asked.

Hannah winced. "They're an hour out. At least."

"Fuck," Linc breathed, and I saw that his hands were shaking.

His woman was in there.

In danger.

A fucking boulder dropped into my gut, and I tried to find something to say that would calm him. But in the end, I didn't say anything. If it were Jess in there, I wouldn't hear any platitudes. The best thing I could do was focus, watch his back in case *his* focus was off, and get us all out of this firefight unscathed.

The chopper banked to the north, mountains and trees coming into view, wilderness swallowing up civilization.

A few minutes later, we'd reached a clearing, and the pilot lowered the bird down enough so that we could jump off. It was gone a moment after we'd hit the ground, moved for cover in the tree lines. I could hear gunfire being exchanged in the distance.

"Closing in on your position," Hannah said into our earpieces. "Status?"

"We've moved," Laila said. "A thousand feet east of the house."

"Roger that."

"Linc?"

Our medic's voice was locked down and icy cold with focus. "Yeah?"

"We're all in one piece," Laila added.

I watched the tension bleed out of my teammate, saw him nod. "Copy."

We took off and began sprinting through the trees, feet silent as we instinctively fell into formation—one at the front (Jess, which made my stomach clench), two in the middle, then two at the rear.

Jess was fast as hell, though her pace was slowed by needing to check the GPS on this unfamiliar terrain.

I could feel Linc's energy roiling under his skin, but he didn't say anything.

Last thing we wanted to do was stumble upon the enemy and blow this extraction, causing someone to get hurt. Luckily, Jess was quick at doing what needed to be done, and each stop was as short as it could be before we were on our way again.

We slowed our pace when voices and gunshots grew louder, circling the clearing, trying to get a line of sight.

Laila's team had taken up behind a ramshackle hunting lodge, barely two walls of it left standing, a huge boulder in the front yard that was almost bigger than the cabin itself.

"We're here," Hannah said. "East side in the trees. We'll circle around, take up supporting positions."

Laila's voice was steady. "Roger that."

With rapid hand movements, Hannah divvied us up, sending me and Jess around the back of the building to cover the rear, Linc to move in closer, probably so he could lay eyes on Olive and see she was safe. She and Lily would take up perimeter positions.

The sun was setting, and we used the shadows to our advantage, creeping closer, dodging the fallen trees and roots and rocks.

I watched Linc dart to the cabin, take up position next to Olive.

He kissed her soundly on the lips and then trained his gun in the direction of the trees.

Risking a glance at my watch, I saw that our rendezvous with the other team was still a half hour off. Bullets continued flying, and whoever was out there was well-armed. They didn't conserve anything, just continued assaulting the cabin with a hailstorm of shots, and though they had to have seen us moving into position to help Laila and company, none of the bullets fired had been trained on us during the approach.

The space around the house grew quiet, and my skin prickled, knowing we were missing something here.

"Hannah?" I whispered into the com.

"I don't know," she whispered back.

My eyes met Jesse's and she shrugged, shook her head, but I could see that she had that same sensation.

The notion that things were about to go FUBAR.

That was when I heard the rumbling.

CHAPTER TWENTY-FOUR

Jesse

I TORE my eyes away from Leo's and squinted at the tree line, trying to see what the source of the rumbling was.

But it was nearing dark, dusk having settled over the mountains, and it was hard to discern more than shadows.

The reverberating grew louder.

My stomach clenched . . .

Just as a huge metal monstrosity burst out from the trees. It resembled a Humvee, but smaller, like an armored ATV, able to navigate the forest floor . . . and it drove straight toward us.

Laila retreated as it barreled into the wall, knocking several of the logs out of place and sending them tumbling toward the agent. Ryker grabbed her by the waist, yanked her behind a portion of the chimney as the ATV retreated then accelerated forward.

"Fall back," she ordered, as it plowed into the wall a second time, sending it tumbling around them, the logs colliding with the ground in an almost deafening fashion.

Olive and Linc peeled off as we covered them.

Ava and Dan followed.

Then finally, Ryker and Laila.

"Go!" I told Leo, knowing I had the better cover, knowing that it went against his every instinct to leave me, but he didn't protest, just took off for the tree line while I peppered the ATV with bullets to buy him time and space.

"We've got you, Jess," Hannah said. "Move, now."

No hesitation.

Just keeping my head down and sprinting for the cover of the trees.

Bullets *pinged* behind me as I zigzagged, *thunking* into the trunks, causing dirt and rocks to explode up around my feet.

And then I was next to Leo, back in the cover.

"How the fuck do they keep finding us?" Laila snapped, her back to a tree, reloading her gun and turning back to the cabin, now crumbled into a heap of timber and stone.

"I don't know," Hannah said, doing the same. "But it's fucking pissing me off."

Ava was on her belly, her rifle pointed across the clearing, each shot careful and measured. "Something's happening."

Yes, it was.

The ATV slid to a stop, its lights shining toward us, blinding me—and I assumed the rest of us—temporarily. I squinted, watched as its passenger door opened, and . . .

Daniel stepped out.

Laila cursed.

Ava fired a shot, but Daniel had apparently been anticipating that. It ricocheted off a clear barrier I hadn't been able to see beforehand.

"Tsk. Tsk, Ava," he said. "Don't think I've forgotten you. Come out, and let's see how good your aim is." He spread his arms. "I'll even give you a clear shot."

Two *pops*, one after another in rapid succession.

A *ping-ping* as they collided with the barrier just over his heart, on his head.

"What the hell is that?" Olive said.

"It's bulletproof," Ava muttered, squeezing off another shot, this one bouncing off the barrier, directly over Daniel's crotch. "That's the only thing I can tell you."

Daniel smirked. "Such a temper." He lifted his voice. "Where's my good friend, Laila? I know she's got to be around, she never lets the little killer, Ava, have too much leash."

"How long until the support arrives?" Laila asked, instead of engaging.

Hannah paused, glanced at her watch. "They should be approaching the property and radioing in five—"

An explosion rent the air.

My gaze immediately went to the clearing, but I knew instantly that the blast had come from some distance away.

Hannah's voice took on an edge of panic. "Red team, pull back immediate—"

Boom.

My heart sank. This one was closer and from the south.

"Red team, report in," she said and waited, no answer on our earpieces. "Blue team. Report."

The silence was sickening.

"They won't be reporting on anything," Daniel called. "Not unless there's an encrypted signal straight from hell.

Fury danced a fiery path down my spine.

Daniel stood in the clearing, glowing in the headlights of the ATV, a smirk on his face that told me he was either seriously deranged or he just had no moral compass. Hannah had ignored him, was still trying to make contact with our backup, even though we all knew what had happened, what the fucker who'd betrayed KTS had done to them.

"Don't you know by now, sweet, delicate Hannah, that I can hear you?" He tapped his ear.

"That's impossible," Ava murmured, and I silently agreed.

The signals we used to communicate were supposed to be technology that couldn't be picked up by surrounding radios, not like normal radio broadcasts or cell phone calls. They were transmitted via biometrics and satellites only KTS had access to, encrypted on both ends without any recorded backups that could later be hacked and listened to. In fact, we supposedly had the most secure communication system on the planet, newly developed with fresh safeguards, since we'd had the issue with Jack slicing our previous one to ribbons.

And yet, Daniel was apparently listening in. *Had* been listening in, if he knew where our backup had been approaching from.

Listening in as though we hadn't completely dismantled and reworked our communications system.

But how?

He tugged out an earpiece, and even from the distance between us, I knew it was one of ours.

Fucking hell. Because seriously, *how?* Had he closed the weapons deal while I was recovering and gotten his hands on the tech? If so, who amongst us was working with him? Who was continuing to betray us, over and over again? And who was betraying us while remaining consistently under the radar?

Questions I'd had over and over the last months.

Questions I'd fucking worked my ass off to discover the answer to.

Questions that I *hadn't* answered, and because of that, we were in this fucking situation.

"This has saved me a lot of trouble." Daniel grinned, slipped the earpiece back in. "And made me richer than a fucking king." His lips curved further. "No, it's *made* me a king." Laughter filled the air.

Laughter that had me reaching for a blade at my hip and launching it forward.

It glowed silver as it spun through the air approaching Daniel, and—

I held my breath.

It bounced off the barrier, landing on the ground by his feet.

"This isn't the movies, Jesse baby," he said, stepping forward and picking it up, twirling it over his fingers. "Nice blade, though." He slid it into his belt. "I think I'll keep it as a souvenir."

I wanted to launch myself across the clearing to see if his shield would be able to stop me up close, but we were in a dangerous place here, and we needed to focus, to figure out an exit strategy.

"We need to move," Laila said.

Ryker nodded, and I just barely heard him say, "We should head back to the house, at least we'd have a secure location to mount a defense until we can get someone in here for extraction."

Laila nodded. "You lead, I'll bring up the rear."

Ryker brushed his knuckles over her cheek. "I love you," he said, making my heart squeeze. He'd never been a tender man, at least not until I'd seen him with Laila, and to see the big lug be sweet, even in a moment like this, with the world going to hell all around us, filled me with a determination to get us all out of the other side of this.

They'd found someone worth living for—Laila and Ryker, Dan and Ava, Linc and Olive—and I wasn't going to accept a world where they didn't have each other. I wasn't going to accept a world without Leo or Hannah or Lily.

I didn't give a fuck who Daniel was, what he was a *king* of.

We needed to survive this night.

Leo squeezed my arm. "Let's go."

Hannah was behind us, Lily and Linc and Olive in front with Ryker.

"Wait," I said, reaching into my duty belt, setting a timer on the small explosive that would create noise and smoke and hopefully enough distraction for us all to get back to the house, even with Hannah and Laila bringing up the rear.

I handed it to Hannah. "Push that, roll it into the clearing, and haul ass," I told her. "You'll have fifteen seconds to get some distance."

She smiled, nodded. "You're the shit, you know that?"

"I'm coming to recognize that," I said lightly. "Be careful and run fast."

"On it." A beat. "Go."

Leo and I took off, running behind the others, and though my attention was on our surroundings and on any threat they might present, in my head, I was counting down from fifteen.

Nine. Eight. Seven.

Our feet pounded. We weren't trying to be quiet. We were going for speed and distance.

Six. Five. Four.

I saw the lights of the house come into view, and we picked up our pace.

Three. Two.

"Come on, Hannah," I breathed.

One.

The world exploded into a cacophony of noise just as we reached the bottom step of the front porch, and I risked a glance back, seeing the smoke rising from a half mile away, lights flashing.

"This way," Ryker said, tugging me inside, his eyes on the trees. "Secure the space."

I joined the others in blocking the doors with as large of furniture as we could move, closing the blinds and pulling the curtains. I'd just secured an exit that led down to the basement when I heard feet pounding on the porch and turned to see Laila and Hannah burst through the front door, Ryker on their heels.

Their chests heaved, but they were in one piece.

Linc and Leo shoved an armoire and blocked the entrance. Ryker, Ava, and I ran around the house, flicking off lights.

"You two, okay?" Olive asked, as we all moved back toward each other.

They nodded, and I watched Hannah's lips press flat. "I

swear that was too easy," she said, her gaze scanning the space. "It was almost as though they let us go."

Dan—Ava's Dan—was checking the phone but shook his head when Laila asked if they had a signal. "No, it's either been cut, or the service is out."

"Anyone have any bars?" Hannah asked.

I pulled my phone out, saw that I didn't have any signal there, either, listened as everyone else said they were in the same boat. "What the fuck?" I whispered. We had a lock on our own system of satellites. We should have a signal. *Always*. That we didn't was . . .

Fuck.

How were we going to get out of here?

I saw the lights before anyone else did, flashing through the curtains, illuminating the interior of the house for one brief flicker.

"Down!" I said.

We all moved, taking cover in case bullets started flying, but none came. At least, not for the moment.

"Three cars," Ava said, her rifle positioned in a tiny corner of exposed glass. Rumbling that grew louder. "And that fucking ATV."

I'd sunk down behind the couch, my eyes catching on something that was beneath the frame of it—

Something flashing.

"Why did you guys leave the house in the first place?" I asked quietly.

A beat then Laila asked, "What?"

"Why did you meet us at the cabin instead of here?" I clarified. "Why not stay here, where it's more secure?"

"We never made it in," Laila said. "We were met with too much fire and couldn't hold our position. We tried to make it around back to find some cover, but we were cut off and didn't even make it halfway there before we were forced to retreat."

To the cabin.

I pulled out my knife. "And then they allowed us to come back here," I murmured.

"What are you thinking, Jess?" Leo asked.

I turned, began sawing at the back of couch, yanking the fabric down as I moved my blade.

"They prevented you guys from getting in here, and then they just let us leave a position where they had us at a disadvantage to come set up something more secure here?" I shook my head, kept sawing at the back of the cushion. "That doesn't make sense."

"No," Hannah said, "it doesn't."

The final bit of fabric gave way, and I hissed out a breath. "And now, I know why."

Leo leaned over, saw what I'd revealed hidden inside the couch, and cursed.

"What?" Hannah asked.

I opened my mouth to explain . . . but that was the moment the bullets began flying.

CHAPTER TWENTY-FIVE

Leo

GLASS SHATTERED.

Bullets sank into walls and furniture.

And I was behind the couch with Jess watching the numbers count down on a bomb that was big enough for me to understand that unless she defused this bomb, we were completely and utterly fucked.

"What do you need?" I asked.

Her eyes met mine for a flash, then she turned back to the bomb, pulling out a screwdriver and undoing the bolts that kept the timer in place. "You need to get everyone out."

"I'm not leaving you."

Tears in her blue eyes. Terror on her face. "There's not enough time. You have to get them—"

I gripped her jaw. "Shut up and tell me what you need to diffuse this thing."

"Go," she whispered, a tear sliding down her cheek. "Please, just go."

"None of us are leaving," I snapped, my tone probably too harsh, but knowing that Jess needed to focus, that with a bomb this size, we wouldn't get far enough to be out of the bomb's radius, even if we left right now. "So, get that fucking thought out of your mind and tell me what you need."

Her eyes closed for a moment.

Then they flashed back open, her hand dashing across her cheek, wiping that tear away. "Light and quiet," she snapped back.

I grabbed my flashlight, shined it where she was working. "I can help you with one but not the other."

A huff.

A roll of her neck, her gaze focusing on the bomb.

"What is it?" Hannah called.

Jesse didn't answer her, probably couldn't bear to. Instead, she was running her fingers lightly over the wires—all black— her lips moving as she silently formed words. I didn't know what she was saying, I couldn't make the bullets stop flying, but I *did* know that I could at least help her by answering Hannah's question.

I caught our team leader's eye, used hand signals to indicate what Jess had found.

Her face didn't change except for her lips going flat, and then she turned to Ava, passed on the information, who then did the same, and in less than a dozen seconds, both teams knew.

Which was, I knew, the amount of time we had left on the timer.

Twelve. Ten.

No time to even get out, never mind the blast radius. We wouldn't even have a chance to make it to the windows or doors.

Nine. Eight. Seven.

Jesse pulled out another knife, still running her fingers over the wires.

Six. Five. Four.

She grabbed one wire, placed the knife beneath it, started to tug upward.

Three. Two.

She pulled the knife out, slid it to the side, put it beneath a different wire, and . . .

I closed my eyes, waited for the world to explode. Instead, bullets kept on flying, glass continued to shatter. I should have trained my gun back outside the house, but all I could do was turn to Jess, wrap my arms around her, and haul her against my chest.

"I love you."

Her mouth fell open.

And even though we were basically fucked, even though I didn't see how we'd possibly get out of this, I kissed her.

Because I could lose her in a second.

From a bullet, a wrong wire, a slippery road, a mistimed fight.

I could blink and not have her any longer.

So, I was going to grab on to her, on to any part of her that I could get, and I wasn't ever letting go—even if I only had her for the next few minutes.

I released her mouth, my chest heaving, her breaths rapid gusts coating my lips with damp heat. She smelled of mint and Jesse, and I almost kissed her again. "I love you," I told her again.

Wide eyes. "Did you just say that?" she breathed.

I smiled, somehow despite the circumstances, I felt my lips curve. "Twice," I whispered, cupping her cheek.

"Leo," she whispered back. "I—"

Linc dropped a magazine to the floor, making us both jump and refocus on the circumstances around us. "I'm almost out."

Lily's voice was grave. "Me, too."

Laila and Ryker exchanged a look that I didn't miss, one that told me they were in no better a position, even as Ava continued firing, switching windows, and conserving her ammo. Hannah

LEVELING THE FIELD   157

had propped herself against a banquet, wasn't firing, which told me enough about the state of her supplies.

"Here," Jess said, handing me three magazines.

I slid them to Hannah, to Laila, and Ryker. Pulled one out of my pocket to toss to Dan, who was mirroring Ava's movements through the house, covering her as she shifted positions, two more to give to Olive, where she and Linc were holed up in the kitchen. They all reloaded, but we were on dredges, and because Ava's rifle was a different caliber, nothing Jesse or I had could help her reload.

"Should one of us try to get out, gain some distance in order to make a call?" Olive asked.

Hannah considered that then shook her head. "We don't know the enemy's numbers, and we're too far from civilization to make any difference."

"We can't just sit here and wait to die," Laila growled. "We've got to do something."

"You have a fucking cell tower handy?" Hannah asked, voice sharp.

Laila released a sharp breath through her nose. "Dan," she snapped, "start looking around for some supplies, anything we can use for weapons, for a distraction. If one of us is getting out of here, we're all going to get the fuck out of here."

Hannah's tone was just as severe. "Olive, help him. Lily—"

"Wait," Jess said, and I watched her face change.

This wasn't a woman who would ever make herself small again, wouldn't back down from a fight, or run scared.

"I have an idea."

CHAPTER TWENTY-SIX

Jesse

"Careful," I breathed as we carried the bomb toward the front of the house.

Leo slowed, and we continued to cautiously make our way into position.

Then just as carefully set it down onto the plastic car, red and small with yellow wheels, the kind a toddler would ride in, and Lily secured it in place with a cord she'd torn from a lamp. Leo glanced at me when we'd released it, after ensuring it was steady and the cord had done its job.

"You ready?" he asked.

I nodded.

He turned, studying the interior of the house, and my eyes had adjusted enough that when I followed his gaze, I could easily see Lily as she returned to stand next to the door, Dan and Ryker there, too, preparing to move the armoire that was currently blocking the fuckers outside from barreling their way in through it. Laila was directly in front of Leo and me, the final two of my homemade flash-bangs in her hands, her thumbs poised over the red buttons that would start their countdowns. I

LEVELING THE FIELD   159

could see Hannah crouched near a window to the side of us, her final magazine inserted in her gun. Ava was behind us, lying on the floor near the back door, her rifle set up in front of her, Olive and Linc standing next to her and ready to remove the blockade there.

Bullets continued to hit the side of the house. They'd never really stopped, and the bright flashes from their guns paired with the lights from the ATV and the vehicles outside continued to wreak havoc with my night vision. It made it difficult to dodge those that still made it through the windows and frames, sinking into the furniture and putting us all at risk.

I met Hannah's gaze, hoping to fuck that this plan would work. She nodded, grinned like we weren't all about to do something that was incredibly dangerous and possibly—no, *actually*—quite stupid.

But no one had come up with a better plan.

So mine—the one with a snowball's chance in hell of getting us out of here alive—was what we were going with.

Because . . . fuck it all.

I was either going to die getting hit by a stray bullet, killed by the fuckers outside when they realized we'd run out of ammo and decided to force their way in, or worse, I'd have to watch my teammates get taken down, see *Leo* get hurt.

We had no way of contacting base.

We had no way of knowing if they'd get here in time, if they'd even be able to get beyond Daniel's men if they did make it.

And . . . I proposed the only thing I could think of, even though it was risky, and I could only hope that we would all be in one piece at the end of this because I wanted my friends to live, and because . . . I really, *really* wanted to have Leo's cock inside me.

Such an inappropriate thought, but at least it relieved the tension heavy on my shoulders, the responsibility bearing down on me that came from coming up with the plan. So, I was going with it.

If aching for Bone Town focused me enough to get us all out of this, then so be it.

"Jess?" Leo asked. "You ready, baby?"

I found his hand, squeezed it tight.

Leo smiled, as though he could see the need for him in my eyes. And maybe he could. Despite the flashes outside, my night vision had adjusted enough that I could study the fierce lines of his jaw, the stubble on his cheeks.

And before I gave the signal to commence this suicidal plan, I knew I needed to say something else. To tell him—

"I love you, too."

The air around us froze. Leo's jaw dropped open, his hands coming to my cheeks.

Then Hannah began to chuckle. "A hell of a time, Jess. A hell of a time."

I only had eyes for Leo, and I could see the emotion in the depths of his gaze, see what my words meant to him. "The perfect time," he said, brushing his mouth across mine, a fucking bomb strapped to a child's toy between us, and knowing that our life would never be normal.

But it would be whole.

Pulling back, he ran the backs of his knuckles over my cheek. "Ready, now?"

My lips turned up. I nodded once.

And then I rolled my shoulders and said, "Let's do this."

Leo pulled back, crouching near the toy car as Laila began counting down. "Three, two, one . . . *go!*"

Hannah began firing, drawing the eyes outside her way, just as Dan and Ryker moved as one, sliding the armoire back enough for Lily to open the door a couple of inches. Laila pressed the button on the devices, slid into the gap, and tossed them carefully across the porch so they rolled toward the contingent of men in front of the house.

Then the door was shut silently again, the armoire back in place as we all counted down. Hannah stopped firing, saving her bullets.

Fifteen seconds passed . . . and *boom*.

The flash-bangs exploded and Dan, Ryker, and Lily *moved*. The armoire was dragged back, the door pulled wide, then the armoire shoved forward, the three of them pushing it hard enough so it toppled onto its front, forming a ramp over the stairs and toward the men out front.

"Go!" Leo said as smoke began filling the house, and I knew we had to act fast before the fog got too thick and Ava lost her chance at a clear shot.

Laila and company sprinted by us, Hannah following them just as a hail of bullets flew toward us, not aimed, but fired in panic. Which made them easy enough to avoid as we stayed low, darted forward, and—

Shoved the bomb down the makeshift ramp.

Leo grabbed my hand the moment it was rolling down the armoire, the bomb flying toward Daniel and his men. He yanked me toward Ava and the rest of our teams. The blockade had been removed from the back door, the wooden panel open, and cover fire was being laid down. We sprinted for the retaining wall, jumping behind just as I heard the *bang* from Ava's rifle.

The world seemed to go still, and every muscle in my body tensed as I waited.

A flash.

I glanced behind me and saw fire and light before the house shuddered, its roof exploding, shards of wood and glass and metal flying in all directions, seeing Ava and Dan sprinting toward us, diving over the lip of the retaining wall . . . just as the force of the explosion hit us.

Illuminated by the fire behind us, I saw their bodies fly forward, landing in a heap on the ground, and neither moved. I crawled toward them, seeing Ava's eyes closed and blood dripping down Dan's temple just as the sound wave hit.

The *boom* was loud.

Louder than anything I'd ever heard, making my ears ring before everything went silent.

I knew the world hadn't grown quiet, only my ears from the explosion, and I turned back to Dan and Ava, saw that Olive was already next to them, smelling salts under Ava's nose, her lids fluttering open. Linc pressing a bandage to Dan's temple.

My ears were ringing now, sounds slowly ebbing back in.

Dan sat up, Ava brushing off Olive to do the same beside him.

Their mouths were moving, but I couldn't yet discern the words.

The earth shook, taking my focus from them, and I turned, just in time to see the house collapse in on itself.

A hand clamped onto my shoulder, and I stood next to Leo, feeling everyone else do the same. We all knew that we had a limited window to get back to the front of the house. Daniel would expect us to run, would be able to chase us down.

But we were done running.

Today, we were going on the offensive.

CHAPTER TWENTY-SEVEN

Leo

WE ALL SPLIT UP, relying on hand signals from Hannah and
Laila to stay organized because our hearing was still shit,
though it was coming back enough for me to hear the splin-
tering of the wood as the house continued to crash down, the
trees surrounding it that had been caught up in the blast crack-
ling with flames.

I bent to grab a gun from one of Daniel's men that we'd
taken down in our run for the retaining wall, saw the others
gather what they could as we rounded the house and prepared
for a firefight.

The metal was warm in my hands, different from the
composite material our weapons were composed of, and
whether it was from the man's body or the blast, I didn't know.
I also didn't care. Not when we were approaching the front
yard and none of us had any idea if the bomb had been effective
against Daniel's shield.

Jess was behind me at my right shoulder, Hannah was even
with me, Lily trailing. Linc had joined with Laila's team,

keeping an eye on Ava and Dan as they circled around the other side of the house.

We crept forward, taking as much cover as we could as we moved, slowly making our way toward the front of the now-destroyed home.

But I don't think any of us were ready for the sight that greeted us.

The utter destruction.

Trees were broken in half, every leaf torn from their branches, resembling toothpicks more than resilient hardwoods.

The yard was scorched, no greenery in sight, just dirt and blackened earth . . . and bodies all around. I caught a flicker of movement, saw it was Laila and company emerging from the other side of the house. She and Hannah communicated briefly via hand signals before we all took off, going over the space that looked like a war zone, checking for survivors, for enemies that might still be in a position to harm us, who would be looking for an opening.

I found no survivors.

And neither did anyone else.

Just prone, unbreathing bodies, the ATV in a twisted heap of metal, and behind them, at the far end of the clearing, the other vehicles were blown clear off their frames, tires in shreds, windows shattered out.

Jess had crouched to pick something up from the crater where the bomb appeared to have detonated when I saw movement.

Not from our team.

But from behind one of the destroyed SUVs.

A flash of metal. A shadow drifting between trees. A gun being lifted.

"Get down!" I yelled, and I was running before I registered moving, sprinting toward Jess. But I wasn't loud enough, or her hearing hadn't yet cleared enough to heed the warning. She started to rise, some piece of metal in her hand, when I heard the gun go off.

Or rather, felt the bullet penetrate my side, beneath my outstretched arms that had been reaching for Jess.

Pain burst to life.

Jess screamed as I tackled her to the ground.

The world went dark.

CHAPTER TWENTY-EIGHT

Jesse

He was dead weight on top of me, pinning me to the ground.

Dead. Weight.

Fuck.

Fuck.

I shoved him off me, rolling him onto his back, searching for the source of his bleed. It was coming heavily, soaking through his clothes and into mine, coating my skin. Finally, I pulled enough fabric and saw his vest had been dislodged, exposing his side. Finding the entry wound, I pressed down hard, cursing and crying and trying to reach into my pack.

"Here."

The voice was near enough to make me jump, having not heard Olive approach.

She handed me a bandage, started tearing into her kit and pulling out supplies. Linc was with her, checking Leo's pulse, taking over for me on the pressure after I'd slammed the covering onto the bullet wound. I didn't want to back up, to let go, was afraid that if I did, then I wouldn't ever get to hold him again.

But I trusted Linc and Olive and knew I had to allow them to do what they were good at.

So, I crouched there with Leo's blood on my hands, willing his chest to continue rising and falling, praying his breaths would keep emerging from his mouth, praying that his eyes would open, and he'd toss that casual, sexy grin in my direction.

Those lids didn't peel back, no matter how hard I silently begged them to.

I stood, glanced back when Olive took my hand, reading her lips more than hearing the words, "He'll be all right."

It was too noisy with the trees blazing, with the ringing in my ears, with my own breathing, and the pounding of my heart drowning out so much else.

He'd saved me.

Like I'd saved him.

I turned in the direction of the trees, where the bullets had flown from, and saw the cluster of my teammates hauling someone out from the shadows.

They dragged him toward me, ignoring his groans of pain, and I saw it was Daniel, his leg clearly broken, blood covering one side of his face.

"You fucking bitch," he spat when they dumped him in front of me.

I kicked his foot.

The one attached to his broken leg, and I didn't feel the least bit guilty when he cried out in pain, the sharp sound cutting through the ringing. This man had spent the last years going after everyone I cared about, going after my *family*. And he'd shot Leo.

He was lucky I didn't immediately put a bullet into his head.

I still had a couple of them left in my gun.

I pulled it out, crouched next to him. "Can you hear me?" I asked.

He smirked, reached up and pulled out an earpiece, chucking it to the ground, doing the same with the other ear. "Yes, I can hear you."

"I'm going to kill you," I murmured, tugging out a knife from my sheath. I jabbed it into his thigh, ignoring the short scream, the trickle of blood, the way his face went pale. "Slowly and painfully and inch by inch by *inch*."

A hand gripped mine, tugging the knife out of his leg. "Enough," Hannah said. "We need to get him back to base, and then I'll let you have a turn with him."

I inhaled, tried to control the rage swirling inside me.

He'd hurt the man I loved. He'd betrayed us. He'd—

My fingers cramped on the knife I still held and though it was tempting to see what I could do to get him to spill his guts about who he'd been working with, I knew Hannah was right. Hands shaking—from controlling that fury rather than terror—I wiped the blade clean on his leg.

His broken leg.

I took a page out of his book and just smirked, even as his scream filled the clearing.

Then I shoved my knife back into the sheath and turned away, knowing we needed to get Daniel under lock and key, needed to use anything in our arsenal to get him talking.

And we needed to get Leo back to base.

That meant I had to find us an exit.

Reaching into my pocket, I yanked out my cell, and though the screen was shattered, the bomb must have taken out whatever had blocked us before because I had a signal.

I called into the base's S.O.S. line, got the chopper en route for Daniel and Leo, a new rendezvous for us with a second chopper, and turned away from the bastard in front of me, of the man I wouldn't hesitate to kill if he didn't prove to be useful.

Laila, Ryker, and Hannah had set up a perimeter with Dan and Lily.

Ava was standing guard over Daniel.

There was nothing left to be done for the moment, so I went over to Leo, and I held his hand, breathed a sigh of relief when I stared down at the man who'd made himself at home in my heart, the man whose eyes were now open, though pain was written across his face.

"I love you," I said.

He smiled, let his eyes slide closed. My pulse skipped a beat, but I just held tight because his chest still moved, his heart was still beating, and his grip on my hand didn't loosen as the minutes crawled by.

The sound of the chopper reached my ears.

But I didn't relax, not until Leo and Daniel were loaded on board, Hannah shoving me on alongside Ava, Linc, and Olive before the rest of the teams left for the second rendezvous point.

I didn't relax until we'd reached the base, Leo was in the infirmary, Daniel was locked up in the brig with Ava to keep guard.

I didn't relax until the second chopper landed and Hannah, Laila, and everyone else had made it safely back onto base.

I didn't relax until Leo was out of surgery, almost twelve hours later, Linc and Olive and the rest of the infirmary staff having seen him through the other side of internal bleeding and a bullet tearing through his insides.

I didn't relax until he was out of critical care and sleeping peacefully in a hospital bed.

Only then did I finally collapse.

But I still didn't relax.

We'd be okay.

Thank God, we'd be okay.

CHAPTER TWENTY-NINE

Leo

I WOKE SLOWLY, a heavy weight on my legs, a bright light shining in my eyes.

Linc was the source of the bright light.

Jess was the source of the weight on my legs.

She looked horrible, black circles marring the space beneath her eyes, her freckles seeming abnormally dark against her pale skin. Her ponytail was askew, hanging shaggily down her back as she slept propped forward in her chair, leaning against the bed with her arms crossed over my shins.

Linc's voice was quiet as he pocketed the flashlight. "First time she's slept in near on three days," he said. "I'd nearly restrained her and drugged her to force her to rest, but then she finally passed out."

"Three days?" I rasped.

Linc helped me drink some water, and the fire in my throat abated.

"You *had* to get shot where you didn't have any body armor, didn't you?"

"Apparently," I said, shifting slightly against the bone-deep ache.

"Shit bounced around in there," Linc said. "We had to do some serious work to get you patched up."

"Jess was okay?" I asked. "Not hit?"

"Scratches and bruises, nothing serious. No one was seriously hurt besides you." A beat. "Well, besides you and Daniel. I set the fucker's leg myself."

I jerked, pain lancing through me at the action, but that wasn't what had me immediately freezing. No, I went statue because my lurching had Jess shifting on my legs, and the last thing I wanted was to wake her when she'd finally found sleep. I met Linc's eyes. "Daniel's alive?"

A nod. "Unscathed except for a broken leg," he said. "Laila's having him sit tight, hoping he'll get tetchy until we interrogate."

"Who's on guard?"

"One of us at all times."

"Good," I said, in approval.

He lifted a syringe. "Yup."

"What are you doing?" I asked.

"Speaking of rest, you need more."

"I'm fine—" He stuck the plastic nozzle into the port on my IV. "I don't want to sleep—"

"Go to sleep, little one," he sing-songed.

I narrowed my eyes. "Don't hit that plunger."

He depressed it anyway, and I felt the slight sting of the medicine enter my vein, the pain that had crept in during the conversation fading, my eyelids feeling heavy.

They dragged down.

I went under.

———

EVEN WITH OLIVE'S special healing compound and all of KTS's medical tech, it wasn't until four days later that I had managed to sit behind the double-sided mirror that looked into the room where Daniel was being held.

He was handcuffed to a bed, his leg in a cast.

I looked to Olive, who'd only allowed me off bed rest if she could push my ass here in a wheelchair and then back to my quarters again the moment I looked peaky—her word, not mine. At least she'd relented two days before to allow me into my own room. Now, if only I could convince Jess to sleep next to me instead of the cot she had brought in.

I was desperate to hold her in my arms.

But she'd refused, not wanting to hurt me.

Damn stubborn woman. I fucking loved her so much.

Through the glass, I watched Daniel shifting on the bed, his cast awkward and unwieldy. I glanced at Olive. "Weren't you working on a rapid bone-healing product?"

She sniffed. "Like I'd waste it on him."

"I was thinking more like he'd be a great guinea pig."

Olive's lips quirked. "You make a good point."

Lily and Hannah were in with him, Jess manning the recording equipment next to us. She had her headphones on, but instead of looking at the video feed, she was focused completely on the computer in front of her. I noticed it wasn't a KTS laptop and instead appeared to be some standard machine anyone could pick up at any big box store.

She typed rapidly on it.

"What is it?"

Her eyes met mine. "He hasn't given us a thing. For a fucking week, we've been in here, using every trick at our disposal, but he hasn't slipped up once."

That wasn't a surprise.

We were trained in counter-interrogation techniques.

Taught to withstand all sorts of psychic manipulation.

He wouldn't be easy to break, especially when he basically

had the playbook for how we operated. It's why he'd been so successful, why it had been such a struggle to get ahead of him. He knew everything about us.

But we knew him, too, knew that at some point we'd find the lynchpin to get him to move.

"But I think . . ." Jess continued typing, fingers clicking on the keyboard. "I think he might have just given us something."

I studied Daniel's face for any indication that he might have felt like he'd fucked up, but the man was just as relaxed as he'd been standing in that clearing seemingly having every advantage—a bomb inside, copious weapons pointed into the house, just waiting for us to either be blown up or to be mowed down.

He smirked at Lily, yawned, and reclined back on the bed, his arms crossed.

As though he were bored.

Or . . . just biding his time.

My nape prickled. I wanted to think I was wrong, but I didn't think I was. A certainty filled my gut. Daniel was going to delay and draw this out until his contacts inside KTS here got him out.

"Fuck," I whispered.

"What is it?" Olive asked.

"I'll wait until Lily and Hannah are back in here." They seemed like they were all but done. Same as everyone else, they weren't getting anywhere in that room. We needed to regroup.

We needed . . . to set a trap.

"Moldova!" Jess exclaimed.

I shifted my gaze away from the room and onto the woman in my heart. "What about Moldova?" I asked.

"He was taunting Laila about a mission there earlier," Jesse said. "But Laila didn't bite, and I didn't understand until I pulled up the mission files. It took me fucking forever, since I was trying to access them via that—" She pointed at the laptop.

"Speaking of which, why are you using *that?*" I asked

lightly. "I'm sure the tech guys could get you any computer you want."

"I don't want any computer. I want one that's fresh and untouched by our guys."

Ah.

"What do the mission files say?" Olive asked.

"That Laila was never there," Jess said. "She was on a mission with Ryker's team before they were together."

My brows rose. "So, who was there?"

I saw a glimmer of a smile—the first I'd seen since I'd awoken in the infirmary—but it wasn't amusement necessarily. It was predatory.

"Who?" I asked again.

"See for yourself."

I glanced at the screen, read the list of five names, and smiled.

CHAPTER THIRTY

Jesse

LEO and I went back to his room after we'd shown Olive, Hannah, and Lily what we'd found.

We'd research the agents.

Track them down.

And then we'd move in.

What we *wouldn't* be doing was leaving Daniel unattended. Laila and Ryker and Hannah would all be quietly calling in favors from their trusted contacts. We'd move on all the targets we identified simultaneously, and we'd get some fucking answers.

But for now, we couldn't let anyone know that we had a lead.

We didn't want the rats scurrying for cover.

The moment that door to the surveillance room closed, Leo hopped out of the wheelchair that Olive had insisted on, snagging the laptop from my hands and starting toward the sleeping quarters.

"What are you doing?" I exclaimed.

He glanced back over his shoulder. "Walking."

My teeth clicked together. "You're supposed to be *riding*."

Slowing, he held a hand out. "Come on, baby," he said, side-stepping the wheelchair when I pushed it toward him. "Let's go to bed."

Stubborn man was tired.

Why he didn't just use the wheelchair was beyond me, but I wasn't going to delay him getting his rest any further. I simply parked the chair, took his hand, and walked back to his room with him.

I touched his cheek when he paused with his hand on the pad, the lock *clicking*, the door sliding open. "I'll see you in the morn—*ah!*"

He swept me up into his arms, the door slamming closed behind us, protests tumbling from my lips because the man had just been fucking shot, had survived a multiple hours-long surgery, had been unconscious for three days.

The last fucking thing he needed was to be hauling my ass across his room.

"I'll see you *now*," he said, tossing me on the mattress.

I didn't even bounce before he was on top of me. I couldn't push him off me without risking hurting him . . . and I didn't want to push him off. I liked him on top of me. I loved the heavy weight of him, the hard planes of muscles, the rigid length of his cock pressing between my thighs.

"Leo," I moaned.

His eyes scorched me. "You promised me that the next time you moaned my name, I'd be inside you."

Heat flooded my core.

My thighs clenched around him.

And then his mouth was on mine, his tongue delving deep. He kissed me like he wanted to absorb me into his body, or maybe that's how I felt. Because his mouth on mine made me whole. One hand was in my hair, his other on my ass, his legs between mine and all the gloriousness of him pressing down on me.

My lungs were screaming when he backed away, and I was shaking, straight up trembling from toes to thighs to tummy to fingers, quaking with need, reaching for him again.

I needed his kiss.

He flicked open my jeans and stuck his hand inside, spearing two fingers around my clit, sliding them through my folds, and thrusting them into my pussy.

I screamed.

He kept moving, yanking my shirt up, tugging my bra up.

His mouth was on my nipple a second later, his fingers working my pussy, pleasure flooding through me, taking me dangerously close to the edge with just that little bit of effort. Sparks in a forest fire. Lightning suddenly turning the night sky bright.

"Leo," I moaned.

He groaned, kissing his way across my chest, sucking my other nipple deep, then moving down my torso, yanking his hand out of my pants, tugging my pants down. "I said, I need to be inside you when you do that again."

"Then *get* inside," I snapped, reaching for him.

His chest was a wall of glorious muscle, and I sat up to lick my way across it while his arm hooked around my waist, yanking me to the edge of the bed and depositing me there while he leaned back to shove down his pants, to kick off his shoes.

"Off," I moaned, pushing up his shirt, yanking it up and over his head, forgetting all about his injuries, not that he seemed slowed by them in the least.

He paused to haul it off over his head.

I didn't pause. I was at work on the tight, black boxer briefs.

And thank fuck, they hit the floor, his cock springing free, hard and straight with moisture glistening on the tip. I leaned forward, licked it off.

"Fuck!"

A burst of movement, and then I was launched backward onto the bed, Leo on top of me, his eyes blazing, his jaw tight, sweat sheening his forehead.

His cock nudged my entrance, started to push in.

"Wait," I exclaimed.

He paused, expression sobering. "You don't want to?" he asked, gently cupping my cheek. "Is it too soon?"

Love filled every inch of my soul.

God. He was just so wonderful.

"No, baby," I said and watched his face fall. "No," I hurried to say. "That's not what I meant. No, to the too soon. Yes, to the I want to. I just . . ." I was naked with the man I loved between my thighs, his cock an inch inside me. It would be so easy to just keep going.

But I wasn't on birth control.

"You need a condom," I blurted.

His mouth dropped open, and my lips parted on a disappointed groan when he pulled out and turned toward the nightstand, possessions hitting the floor as he searched through the drawer.

Then he was sighing in relief, or maybe that was me.

Either way, he was tearing the condom open with his teeth, rolling it down the length of his cock, nudging me back. "Tell me you're with me," he said, or maybe begged.

"Get inside me," I demanded, wrapping my thighs around him.

He didn't wait.

He wasn't particularly gentle.

He thrust deep, and I gasped at the intrusion, my pussy clenching, my head falling back. "Leo," I moaned.

"Fuck, baby," he said, stroking into me, fast and steady and driving me perilously close to the edge of pleasure. "That was as good as I imagined." He nipped my bottom lip. "Do it again," he demanded, gripping my ass in one hand, pounding into me, and changing the angle.

Just enough so that every nerve inside me stood up at rigid attention.

My breathing hitched.

I moaned his name again.

And then again.

And all the while, he kept moving, mercilessly driving me up and up and up until my orgasm barreled through me with the force of a Mack Truck.

I was blind. I was limp.

I was a being of only bliss.

"Jess," he groaned, his lips on my neck. My name on his lips sparked another wave of pleasure, my pussy clenching around him, and then he thrusted once, twice more before stiffening, my name tumbling out again and again as he stroked into me until he was spent and limp and collapsed on top of me.

"I love you," he murmured.

"I love—" I froze, reality slowly intruding. I shoved him—as gently as possible—off me. "Oh my God! Your chest. I— Are you hurt?" Panic wove through me, and I spotted my cell on the ground, reached for it. "I need to call Olive. She or Linc need to check you out and make sure—"

His mouth curved.

His arms banded around me, knocking my phone to the mattress. "God, you're beautiful," he rasped, cupping my cheeks.

"Leo—"

A chuckle. "Not until I'm inside you."

My mouth dropped open. *"Leo!"*

Fuck, he was sexy when he smiled like that.

And no sooner had that thought crossed my mind than his mouth was on mine, making the worry drift away, forgetting his injury and Daniel and the other bad guys that were out there.

It was just me and Leo.

Our kisses. Our bodies. Our courage in finding a way out of the darkness. In finding a way to each other.

For now, that was the only thing that mattered.

CHAPTER THIRTY-ONE

Leo

THE KNOCK at the door was insistent.

Jesse finally slept in my arms, and despite the ache in my shoulder from the exercise I probably shouldn't have participated in—twice—but *exercise* I wouldn't ever regret, I felt better than I had in a long time.

No more fear yanking me down into a black hole of what-ifs.

No more thinking about all the things that could go wrong. Because they *could* go wrong, they *had* gone wrong. Everything could change in an instant, and lying to myself about the feelings I had for Jesse wouldn't make a difference.

I loved her.

And even *if* all I felt was friendship, losing Jess would be devastating.

There was a reason I'd come to Georgia, why I'd left my team and joined hers. I couldn't live without her.

So, I wasn't going to.

Luckily, she'd forgiven me because otherwise, I would have had to go on a campaign for her heart, and that might be—

The knock came again, just as I was realizing that I *was* lucky that she'd forgiven me, but also that she deserved her man to campaign for her heart, whether or not I'd already won it. She deserved the romance and caring, and I knew that I owed it to her to prove to the world how much she meant to me.

So that she would never *ever* doubt my love for her.

Carefully, I slipped out of bed, snagged my boxer briefs, and yanked them up, moving to the door and tugging it open before whoever was on the other side could knock a third time.

"Jesse's sleeping," I snapped before I even saw who it was.

Who it was—for the record—was Hannah.

Her brows lifted, her gaze dipping down and back up. She whistled softly. "Damn, Jess did good."

I glared.

She shrugged. "As I've said before. I'm gay, not dead. I can appreciate the pretty."

I snorted, closing the door behind me so my team leader didn't wake up my woman. "What do you need?"

"First"—she inclined her head to the wall, and I saw she'd brought the wheelchair back . . . *joy*—"humor Olive because it makes Linc's life easier." A pause, her hazel eyes waiting for an answer. Stifling a sigh, I nodded. "Second"—those eyes went deadly, demonstrating in a heartbeat why this woman led our team—"if you hurt her again, I will cut your balls off and shove them down your throat."

Jesus, the way her gaze dropped down to my crotch had that particular body part attempting to suck itself back into my body.

But also, I was a fucking KTS agent. I didn't cower from threats, though my hands were clenched into fists at my side, trying to resist the urge to protect my dick from her laser-eyed glare. Instead, I held her gaze and said, "I will destroy anyone who hurts her, even if the fucker who does it is me."

Silence.

Our stares locked.

Then Hannah smiled. "Good."

The door to our section of the sleeping quarters clicked open, and Lily strode through, her face breaking into a smile upon seeing us.

She strode over to me, lifted her hand for a high-five. "You did the deed!"

I snorted, rolled my eyes, even as she grabbed my palm, so it smacked against hers.

"Lily," Hannah warned.

She tossed her ponytail over her shoulder and smirked at Hannah. "I didn't mean them commencing bang o'clock. Which obviously . . ."

Hannah coughed.

Lily cleared her throat. "I meant"—her eyes came to mine, sparkling with humor—"that you finally admitted that you're in love with Jesse."

I narrowed my eyes at her.

She smiled innocently.

"It was your idea to lock us in the conference room, wasn't it?"

Lily blew on her knuckles, buffed them on her shoulder. "Someone needed a push."

"That was more than a push," I muttered, "that was toppling us into a snake pit."

Hannah snorted.

"You weren't any better," I grumbled. "Considering you were texting every minute with advice."

"Well, your dumbass wasn't going to get there alone, was it?"

That was true.

"I can be a little stubborn."

Hannah rolled her eyes. "She didn't want to let you go, you know. Even when she told you to go, she didn't really want it. She wanted you to fight for her, to look into yourself and see that she was your person."

"I know." A beat. "Now."

Lily laughed, slinging her arm around Hannah's shoulders and squeezing tight. "He's the muscle of our team, not the brains."

Chuckles rose in my throat. "I should probably be offended by that—"

"But you're not gonna be." Lily smiled, dropped her arm, and hugged me tight, pressing a kiss to my cheek. "I'm glad you finally got your head out of your ass. I wouldn't want to lose you"—a poke to my middle—"or your abs."

"Because even though you're gay, you still can admire pretty?" I asked wryly.

Hannah clapped my back. "Now you're getting it."

We all burst into laughter, but almost immediately, I began backing into the room. I needed to get back to Jess. I wanted one night without any—*more*—interruptions. "Thank you, guys," I said. "I don't think it would have gotten through my dumb"—I slanted a glare at Lily, who just smirked—"brain without your intervention."

"Well," Hannah said dryly, "considering it took eight KTS agents to plan the mission to bring you two together, I'd say that's true enough."

Lily stage whispered, "You owe us pizza and beer, by the way."

"I will gladly pay up."

"See that you—" Her cell rang, and she pulled it out of her pocket. "Oh, it's my mom! I've got to take this." A kiss to my cheek, to Hannah's, before she bounced down the hall, slapped a palm to the panel by the lock on her door, pushing inside and disappearing.

"She's something else," I murmured.

How she could shift from serious, dangerous agent to cheerful, mischievous cheerleader type defied convention. But I'd seen her on missions, watched her flip that switch in her brain to become deadly and sober, and then the moment the risk was abated, she was right back to mischief and teasing.

She had a light inside her that wasn't unlike Jesse's.

It burned perhaps more overtly, was a force to be reckoned with, but it was the same . . . just as I suspected the way Hannah stared after Lily was very much the way I stared after Jess.

Moths to a flame.

Hannah blinked, and the longing was gone, her no-nonsense face back in place. "Get some rest, take care of my girl, and then be ready to hit it on all cylinders."

"No more interruptions?"

Humor bled onto her face. "Maybe I should barge in at one A.M. demanding you pay up on that pizza and beer, just to be as big of a pain in the ass as you've been since joining my team."

I narrowed my eyes.

"But I won't." A beat. "For Jesse."

"I'll work on getting myself crossed off your Shit List."

Hannah shrugged. "It'll take some serious work."

"The best things do."

Her gaze flicked to Lily's door, her lips pressing flat. Then she met my gaze and nodded before turning for her room. "That they do, Leo. That they do."

CHAPTER THIRTY-TWO

Jesse

THIS WAS the second time I was waking up in Leo's arms.

But it was markedly different from the first.

The warm arms and the spicy scent of him were familiar. The feeling of utter contentedness was not, so I found myself sinking into the moment, soaking it in. We had a lot of work to do, things to work through on both our parts.

But we'd found the courage to have each other.

Which was why I knew I was never going back to the person I'd been before.

Leo's fingers trailed up and down my spine, lightly bumping over the skin covering my vertebrae, making me shiver and shift closer. "You, okay?" he murmured.

"I'm happier than I've ever been."

"Because you got some sleep?" he asked lightly, his fingers dipping lower, tracing over the curves of my ass.

"No," I said, pressing a kiss to his chest.

"Because I gave you orgasms?"

"Hmm," I teased. "They were okay, I guess."

"Just okay?" He slipped his fingers between my cheeks, slid them forward and lightly circled my entrance.

I bit back a moan, my hips jaunting forward.

He coaxed a leg up and over his hip, and I felt the hard length of his cock brushing through my folds. But he didn't slide inside, didn't do anything but stroke gently, the tip of his finger shifting back and forth.

I shuddered. "*Leo*," I moaned.

He nipped my chin. "I warned you about that," he said, the words scorching my skin.

"Then get inside me," I demanded, pushing against his hand, intending to turn for the nightstand and the box of condoms he'd unearthed the night before. But the action had his finger slipping in, and I froze, a groan tumbling off my tongue. "That's not—" I gasped when he pushed deeper, curled it forward and hit that sweet spot inside me. "What I—" A hiss, my mouth finding his, our kiss reducing me to cinders as he stroked me deep and slow and—

Someone pounded on the door.

And I mean *pounded* because our doors were thick, and I was in a state—that state being that Leo was hard and close, my orgasm barreling down on me—so I wasn't exactly aware of my surroundings.

Leo was though, and he muttered, "Ignore them," as he kept stroking.

But the pounding didn't stop.

And unfortunately, it wasn't his cock pounding into me. The door practically rattled on its hinges.

"Just a little more," I moaned. I was so close.

Our cell phones started ringing. Both, right at once.

"Fuck," he snapped, pulling away from me, and though I understood it must be an emergency, I was mentally cursing a blue streak as I jerked Leo's T-shirt over my head and followed him as he stalked to the door.

His ass in those boxer briefs was just . . .

Muah.

He yanked open the door, revealing Hannah on the other side, her expression like granite.

And I knew in an instant that things were fucked.

CHAPTER THIRTY-THREE

Leo

WE GOT DRESSED IN A HURRY.

Ran through the halls.

Even though we knew it wouldn't make a difference.

Olive was kneeling outside the door, next to a pale Ava, blood dripping down her face. Dan was at her side, clamping a bandage to his forearm, the surrounding skin stained crimson.

Jess slid to a halt, and I squeezed her fingers.

"They're okay," Hannah murmured. "They're all okay."

"Except for," Lily began, and my gut clenched, "Daniel."

It didn't stop clenching, but I definitely relaxed a little bit. My teammates were safe, Laila and her team were safe. I stepped forward and peered through the cell door, the lock blown off, scorching the concrete walls around it.

"Fuck," I hissed.

Jesse slid behind me, her front to my back, and I really shouldn't be aware of her breasts pressing into me, the soft, floral scent of her. Not when I was staring at the sight in front of me.

"What happened?" I asked.

Hannah spoke first. "Someone tried to gas those two, but they realized what happened, fought the attacker, and signaled the alarm."

"Who?" I asked, thinking they were lucky they'd gotten the alarm off, otherwise they might have been dead.

"We don't know," Dan said. "They pumped some sort of smoke in. It was like trying to fight through concrete. They knocked me and Ava out, and by the time everyone else came, the room . . . well, Daniel was like that."

I glanced back into the cell where we'd been holding the former agent.

Blood was everywhere, puddles of it on the concrete floor. It was a bizarre thing, how much blood a human body held, and it seemed like every drop from Daniel's body was spread out on the floor. His head lay at an angle, his neck was nearly severed from the force of the slash across it, his brown eyes glassy.

But I could swear there was something like fear frozen on his face.

Fear where I'd only ever seen a smirk.

Who the fuck had done that?

Jesse tugged on my hand. "Come on," she whispered, tugging me back and into the surveillance room. Ryker was at the keyboard, and we moved close to see him pulling up the camera feed then rewinding it.

Pausing to see Jess and me on the screen.

Then back again to see Hannah and Lily peeking in, their faces grim.

Back further. Playing to see Laila and Ryker skidding to a halt, the curse words that had tumbled out of their mouths evident even through the feed.

Back. Play.

We watched Linc dart into the room, smoke clearing in the hall behind him, Ava and Dan prone on the floor. He froze in the opening before turning back, his phone to his ear as he bent toward Dan, Olive already working on Ava.

Back a little more.

"There," Jess whispered, pointing toward the screen.

Ryker rewound it a little further and hit the button to play the recording.

We watched Daniel pace the room, back and forth until he froze, his eyes going to the door. I saw his trademark smirk slide into place, and there was a flash as a small explosion burst open the lock.

The door was pulled wide.

A slender form entered, the hood from their sweatshirt pulled over their face, and I squinted, unable to tell if it was a man or woman. Not tall. Not overtly muscled or curved. A standard androgynous build.

I leaned closer as Ryker zoomed in, trying to see something that would allow us to identify who it was.

Nothing.

They knew where the camera was and kept their face deliberately away. The hoodie was baggy, hiding body shape. They even wore gloves.

Daniel moved toward the person, as though he were just going to walk out of the cell without a care in the world.

The intruder struck.

A knife glinting, tearing across Daniel's throat.

One second, he was cockily heading for the door, the next he was grabbing for his throat, toppling backward and bleeding out on the floor.

The intruder casually stepped over Daniel's body and disappeared.

"Track them through the other cameras," Laila said.

Ryker nodded and started typing, pulling up the feed for the hall, and we watched as the intruder moved through the cameras heading for the yard, still avoiding the cameras . . . until the feed cut.

"What happened?" Laila asked.

Ryker kept typing. "I don't know." He pulled up a camera

on the other side of the yard, and we all searched, but there was nothing but shadows.

"What about the other side?"

Ryker switched to that camera.

Nothing.

"I'll go through them all," he said.

"We need to check the codes and keycards used to get through the doors," Laila said.

I nodded. "I'll get on that."

Ryker had rewound the footage and was viewing what happened in the cell again.

I started to turn for the door, intending to get to work.

"Wait," Jess said. "Back it up—"

My eyes went to the screen, and I saw the person walking down the hall leading to the yard.

"Pause there."

I frowned, not seeing anything this time I hadn't seen the first.

"They took their gloves off."

Blinking, I looked closer, along with Ryker and Laila. "Damn," Ryker said. "You're right."

"Zoom in," Laila said.

But Ryker was already doing that, and we all stared as the grainy image of the hands blew up on the screen. "Let me see if I can clean this up," Ryker murmured, running the image through a program that could fill in the blanks between the pixels.

"What's that?" I asked, pointing to a spot between the person's thumb and forefinger.

"A tattoo?" Jess asked.

"Looks like it," Ryker said, squinting.

Laila rested her hand on his shoulder. "Can you clean it up anymore?"

Ryker nodded, still working on the image.

And we watched as it slowly came into focus.

It seemed like a crescent moon, only there were two smaller images at each point. The photograph wasn't good enough to make them out, though, nor the writing that made up the curved interior.

"Have you ever seen anything like this?" Laila asked.

All of us shook our heads.

Laila sighed, rubbed her temple. "What a fucking mess." She took one moment, chin dropped to her chest, and then Ryker's hand found hers, same as Jess's was in mine. And if Ryker steadied her half as much as Jess did me, then I knew Laila would be okay. "Okay," she said, lifting her head and straightening her shoulders. "I'll meet with Hannah to confirm this, but as of now, can you continue looking into the five agents from Moldova?" she asked Jess.

Jess nodded.

"And you're going to follow up on the codes and keycards?" she asked me.

"Yes," I said. "I'll report to you and Hannah the moment I have anything."

Ryker stood up, slid his arm around Laila's waist. "Why don't you continue with the cameras? I'll take care of . . ."

Laila's face softened. "I should—"

Jess squeezed my hand, and we slipped from the room, hearing Laila say, "I shouldn't care about him. I just don't know how he went so fucking bad. He hurt so many people, hurt *me*. I just—" Her voice broke, and I quietly closed the door behind us.

Hannah and Lily were discussing how to take care of the body, Linc and Olive having shuttled Ava and Dan off to the infirmary to get checked out. Since Hannah had things well in hand, I filled them in with what we'd found and what we planned to get started on.

"Keep me updated," she said, turning to intercept two agents from another team who'd wheeled in a stretcher topped with a body bag.

Jess caught her arm. "You might want to give them a few minutes."

Lily's eyes flared with understanding, and she nodded, moving to the body and crouching by Daniel's left hand. Her head whipped back toward us, and she nodded for a second time.

So, he had the tattoo as well.

Lily came over, rubbing her temple. "I've seen that image before," she said. "I know I have."

My eyes widened. "Where?"

"I don't know . . . a book or—" She broke off and pulled out her phone. "I need pictures of the tattoo. Good pictures."

Jess turned to help her, but I snagged her hand, tugged her back. "Lily's got it."

Her eyes flicked over her shoulder. "I need to see."

Releasing her, I trailed them over to the corpse.

Lily snapped a few pictures and then Jess and I bent close, studying the tattoo that he had inked between his forefinger and thumb. A moon and the writing was . . . "*Quod vero dicitur per comparationem*," I murmured. "What the hell does that mean?"

"The truth is relative," Jess said, and Lily and I looked at her in surprise.

She shrugged. "It's Latin."

More surprise from Lily and me.

Jess lifted her hands in surrender, "Nerd, remember?"

"That nerddom taught you Latin?" Lily asked.

"That nerddom taught me lots of things. For example . . ." She bent closer, murmured, "Those are scales."

"What?" I asked, leaning closer and seeing that the tiny images at each point of the moon were indeed scales. One in solid black at the bottom of the moon, one just outlined in black at the top. "What is this?"

Lily sighed. "I don't know. But I'm going to find out."

"I know you will," Jess said.

We spent a few minutes talking about the scales and what they might mean, but unfortunately, Jess's nerddom didn't cover the meaning of symbols, scales or not, and my dumbass wasn't any help.

Regardless, Lily at least had a place to start, and I knew she wouldn't sleep until she had answers.

With nothing further to do, Jess and I slipped out of the hall and headed toward our offices after a short pitstop to my rooms to grab the laptop she *had* apparently purchased from a local electronics store. "We might need to do the same for all of us, if our systems are compromised."

"Yeah, maybe." She sighed. "But it's not like I have a secure server. I'm accessing KTS's info, so if someone has access to that . . ."

"We might lose our chance at the info anyway."

"Exactly."

She sighed again, and I stroked my hand down her back. "What is it?"

"Every time we seem to be making progress, it's like we get shoved back two fucking steps." She dropped the laptop onto her desk. "We get clues, bits of the story, and none of it makes any difference when agents are at risk out there when they're *dying!*"

Her chin dropped to her chest.

"And every time I think we're getting somewhere, we just end up with more questions." She rubbed her forehead. "It just doesn't seem like we're going to ever sort this out, and—"

Her voice cracked, and I couldn't take it any longer.

I pulled her into my arms, held her close. "It's a shit show. I know it is," I said into her hair. "But we managed to find our way through the shit of our pasts, and we managed to find each other." I cupped her cheek, tilted her head up so I could stare into her damp blue eyes. "And I'm not going to give that up.

I'm not going to give *you* up. So," I said, brushing my lips across hers. "That means that we have to keep going, keep fighting. Even if it seems like we're not getting anywhere."

Her eyes slid closed, her body drifted closer.

"Because we have this family we've made, and we're going to fight for it, fight for our friends, fight for KTS."

"And if it's fucking rotten to the core?" she asked, fingers clenching on my shoulders. "Because it seems more that way, every single day."

"Then we cut out the rot," I said. "We keep searching. We find these fuckers, and we get our place back."

Her expression shifted, going hard, going determined as she nodded. "We're going to get our place back," she said, nodding as she slipped out of my arms. "We're going to make it safe again."

"God, I love you."

"Because I'm weak and considered giving up?"

I cupped her cheek again. "Not weak." I ran my thumb over her bottom lip. "And everyone's determination wavers every once in a while."

"Okay," she said, sitting down at her desk. "How about because I look good in your T-shirt?"

I sat opposite her, opened up my laptop. "That is true. But no."

Her lips twitched. "Because I have an owl named Luna who screeches like a banshee?"

"Nope," I said, staring into her beautiful eyes and thanking every god on the planet for giving me a chance at having her forever. "That's not it, either." Though I knew I would never, *ever* be under the moonlight again and not think of Jesse.

"Maybe because I—"

"Am my heart," I interrupted. "Because I will never *ever* live another moment on this earth and not be thankful that my path brought me to you."

She inhaled sharply.

Then swatted my hand where it rested next to my laptop. "Don't do that!"

I captured her fingers, lifted them to my lips. "Why?"

"Because I need to research like a badass and find out everything I can about the Moldovan Five," she said. "Which means I can't cry."

"Moldovan Five?"

"I've given them a nickname," she said, pink streaking across her cheekbones. "Makes my life easier than saying five agents who once were on a mission in Moldova."

"It works."

She smiled, and I brushed my thumb across one cheek then the other. "Thanks for not making fun of me."

"I love you," I whispered. "Even if Moldovan Five sounds a bit like a bad boy band."

She snorted. "So much for that."

"Jess?"

Her brows lifted.

"You're okay with this?"

The brows arched higher. "Okay with . . ."

"Us?"

"I mean, I thought I'd already made that clear," she said. "I'm done with denying myself what I want, and I want you."

My heart thudded, once, fiercely against my ribs. "We were locked in a room."

"That's true."

I kissed her fingers again. "And then fighting for our lives, dodging gunfire, and rewiring a bomb."

"That's also true."

"And I guess, I just want to make sure that . . ." What? She knew what she was getting into? That she wanted me? That she was okay with how dramatically things had changed between us?

The truth was that she had to be okay with it.

I wasn't leaving her, and I'd do whatever the fuck I had to in order to convince her to keep me, to want me, to prove that I could be the man she deserved.

"Stop."

I blinked.

"Have I given you an indication that I didn't want you?" She made a face. "Putting aside that one time I asked you to leave."

I pressed my lips together. "No," I said. "But also, I feel like I need to reiterate that we were fighting for our lives, and before that, we were trapped together in a room."

"And you're insinuating that because of that, I don't know my own mind?"

"Um, no?"

"So, you think I'm lying to you?"

"Um . . . no?" I said again.

She laughed, pushing up from her chair, rounded the desk, and plunked into my lap. "So then," she said. "That's your answer, baby. I want you. I've been in love with you for years, so fuck yes, I want to see where this goes."

I inhaled.

Her hands came to my cheeks. "Will you do something for me?"

I covered her hands with my own. "Anything," I promised, knowing that I meant it with every single part of me.

"Well, it's for us," she said. "Because I want us to stop punishing ourselves and just be with each other. We're only on this planet for so long, and I'm done being miserable in my life. You make me happy." A shrug. "I want more of that."

"Well then," I said. "Then I want to give it to you." I rubbed my nose against hers. "I'll give you *everything*."

Blue eyes filled with tears, and she sniffed. "Not fair."

"What?"

"You're being sweet again," she mock grumbled. "And I still need to research like a badass."

Laughter bubbled out of me, and I slowly released her. "Then I guess we need to get to work."

Her lips curved. "Yes, we do."

A pat to her bottom. A movement that had her back on her feet, my gaze following her as she crossed around her desk again and sat down. Then I forced myself to look away, to log in to my computer, to start pulling up data about the doors, and then suddenly Jesse's gaze was on mine.

"For the record," she murmured. "I love you. And I know that if I do cry, you'll just wipe my tears away."

My throat went tight and abruptly, *I* was the one fighting tears.

But that was okay.

Because I knew Jess would wipe mine away, too.

CHAPTER THIRTY-FOUR

Jesse

"ARE YOU HUNGRY?" Leo asked, his arms around me.

We were sprawled in bed, naked because that seemed to be the way he liked me.

It was late, nearly two in the morning, and we hadn't rested much for weeks now, had just parked our asses in front of our computers to find out as much information as possible—Leo about base security, me about my Moldovan Five.

The pieces were coming together.

I was tracking down their current locations, as well as going back through old reports and trying to tie them to missions that had gone awry, where other KTS agents or safe houses had been compromised. But they were smart.

They covered their tracks, and their trails weren't easy to follow.

Not if I didn't want to alert them to our having discovered the connection.

Still, I'd begun with Daniel's trail and was slowly making my way through the other four. I thought I was making progress, but I also wasn't holding my breath. Every single time that I thought we had things figured out . . . it all went to shit.

So yes, I felt like I was making some headway.

No, I wasn't going to pretend that headway was going to be the key to solving this fucked up mystery.

Because nothing about what was happening with KTS was straightforward.

No further clues had come from the surveillance footage, even though Leo had spent hours going over every minute of it. He was still going through the door and keycard information. It had initially seemed like it was all erased, but he'd found a backup server for that data and thought he might be able to extract some of the information from there.

All we knew was that they'd wanted Daniel dead.

So they'd had him murdered and made our security look like child's play.

The latter was bad.

The former . . . I mean, I couldn't grieve too much for the bastard, not after all he'd done. So maybe it was less murder and more . . . proper ending. But even with him thankfully wiped from the planet, we hadn't gotten nearly enough from him.

We didn't have answers. Just more fucking questions.

So it was good that Leo had come into my office and closed my laptop, then dragged me off to the cafeteria for a late dinner.

I'd planned on going back to work afterward, wanting to keep diving into the mission files to find out as much as possible.

But he'd coaxed me to my room.

Truthfully, though, it hadn't taken much coaxing.

Not with Leo.

Every day was better than the last. I was settled in a way that I'd never felt, and . . . I trusted him.

"I think that we stuffed ourselves full enough, don't you?" I asked in response to his question about whether or not I was hungry. I couldn't possibly be, not with the amount of food I'd eaten.

He bent, dropped a kiss on the tip of my nose. "Well, *you* happened to lie there while *I* did all the work," he said. "So *I* worked up an appetite."

I giggled. "That, and you're always hungry."

"True." He wrapped his arms around me, tugged me closer, nuzzling into my throat. "Just like how I know you love chocolate cake in the middle of the night."

I loved chocolate cake at any time of day.

But he was right. I loved it especially in the middle of the night. It felt decadent and like I was breaking all the rules.

"Maybe," I hedged.

Because even more than chocolate cake, I loved being able to have Leo in my life, to keep growing our friendship, to share all the little things like cake and Luna, to listen to Leo talk about everything and nothing, to discover how he can't follow the puck during a hockey game on TV and how he never remembered to bring his swim goggles when he hit the pool.

I'd bought him extra pairs.

I'd teased him about needing the blue circle to watch the Gold game properly.

He'd discovered my obsession with after-hours cake.

He pushed up out of my arms and I groaned, reaching for him. "Where are you going?"

Leo didn't stop, just walked his naked and delicious ass over to the small fridge tucked under the counter of his kitchenette and . . . pulled out a slice of chocolate cake.

And one fork.

Ha.

Give the man some credit. He was a smart one.

"Have I told you I love you?" I asked as he set it in my lap.

"Not for at least five minutes," he said, sliding into bed and handing over the fork. "But I'm never going to get tired of hearing you say it."

"Well then," I said, scooping up a bite. "I love you."

He smiled, and it sank into my skin, filled me with such joy that I knew whatever was happening with KTS, with the traitors, with all the fucked-up shit in the world, I would always feel lucky that we'd found each other.

Because life wasn't guaranteed.

Because we'd both been through enough hell to hang onto something good—at least now that we'd gotten out of our own way to figure out exactly how good it could be.

I'd kick Leo's ass if he backtracked.

Just like Leo would gently coax—*ha*—mine back into place.

We had each other.

But finally, I wasn't scared of that connection. Our relationship had filled all those holes inside me, filed away the sharp edges, and made me feel like . . . *me*. Made me feel more than I could have ever dreamed.

It was love.

And I'd discovered that love was the simplest and also the most complicated thing I'd ever experienced.

It was overwhelming. It was wonderful.

It was terrifying and as comfortable as an old, soft hoodie.

It was Leo.

It was me.

It was . . . us.

EPILOGUE

Jesse

THREE MONTHS since Daniel had been murdered, and finally we were moving out the next night.

Hannah, Lily, Leo, Linc, (and seriously, how had I never noticed all those L names before?) and I were flying to Ukraine where one of the agents from the Moldovan Five was stationed, ostensibly as a starting point for a mission to reconnoiter an up-and-coming segment of the Russian mob.

But in reality, we would be bringing him in.

Just as Laila and company would be bringing an agent down in San Francisco, and two other teams hand-picked by Hannah and Laila would be acting concurrently in Puerto Rico and South Africa.

Tonight, however, I was finalizing some details on the mission, trying to prepare for any eventuality.

Daniel was buried.

The backup server Leo had discovered with keypad data had revealed that the person who'd murdered Daniel had used different codes and keycards at each exit—everyone's from mine to Leo's to Ava's—until they'd disappeared. They'd gamed the system, and we still didn't know how. So for now, everything had gone low-tech. Actual keys at the important doors, physical guards at the others.

Not a permanent solution, but we couldn't just rely on a system where someone could just breeze in, murder someone, and then disappear into the shadows.

And I wasn't sure I was going to trust any new tech when it seemed like someone with experience in the department had turned.

The weapons.

The security system.

The missions going wrong.

Agents getting killed.

I worried that we were never going to get to the bottom of it all. I was overwhelmed and stressed and . . . happier than I'd ever been in my life. Because of Leo. Because of how I was with him. Because of how we were together.

Even despite the constant bleary eyes from tracking down the Moldovan Five.

And seriously, my life had come full circle—from bleary eyes to bleary eyes.

I'd just brought along a whole lot of happy with me on the second half of that spherical trek.

Because I'd found courage and heart and my true love along the way.

A knock had me glancing up and then smiling when I saw Leo resting against the doorjamb.

I frowned. "Why are you wearing a suit?"

His mouth curved, and he slowly made his way over to me, spinning my chair so it was backward, and he was crouching between my legs. His hands came down on either side of me, resting on either arm.

He didn't answer my question, just slanted his mouth across mine, kissed me senseless, then tugged me out of the chair.

"Come with me," he murmured.

I blinked but didn't argue, since he'd kissed me senseless. Just stood up and let him drag me from the room, down the hall, and back to my quarters, unlocking the door.

Smiling, I moved inside and froze.

Flameless candles on every surface. Rose petals and floral arrangements, and in the closet, a white, zippered bag hanging on the rail, an envelope pinned to its front with my name on it.

I spun back, but the door was closed.

And Leo wasn't on this side of it.

"What?" I breathed.

My phone buzzed.

The envelope, love.

I tucked it into my pocket, walked numbly over to the zippered bag and opened the envelope.

Because you deserve the fantasy.
And because I'll do my best to always give it to you.
-L

My heart pounded and my eyes stung, and then I lost the battle with tears altogether when I unzipped the bag and saw the sparkling silver dress on the hanger. Even in my dreams, I couldn't have pictured it.

There were even shoes and a box with a gorgeous owl-shaped pendant, sparkling diamonds forming its eyes.

"Oh, Leo," I whispered, running my finger over the charm. He was just so . . .

Wonderful.

When I got myself together, I saw another note on the hanger, telling me to get ready and he'd be waiting.

I released a shaking breath.

It was a fantasy.

It was . . . reality.

Sniffing, I jumped when my phone buzzed again.

Fewer tears and more makeup.

Laughing and shaking my head, I did just that—moving to the bathroom and setting my phone on the counter before taking a shower, shaving *all* the places. I even washed my hair, taking my time to blow dry it and curl it into loose waves. Then I went all out with the makeup.

Because if I was living in my fantasy-reality, I was going for it.

Smokey eyes, a bright pink lipstick, two coats of mascara.

Then slipping into the only lingerie I owned, a pale green lace thong and white stockings, a matching strapless bra. I fastened the necklace around my throat and then stepped into the heels first, instinctively knowing it would be difficult to do so once I got the puffy dress on.

And then that was all I had to do.

Carefully, I slid the dress from the hanger and stepped into it.

There was only one problem.

I couldn't do up the zipper.

So, with my hands holding up the front of the dress, I moved to the door and opened it. Leo smiled as he turned to me . . . and then his jaw dropped open.

Pleasure flooded me, and not just from the heat in his gaze, but from me, from my being happy with my body. I wasn't finding myself lacking. I felt beautiful and feminine and . . . me.

"Can you do me up?"

Heat turned to an inferno as I watched his throat work as he attempted to swallow. Then he slipped behind me and slowly did up the zipper, the rough calluses on his fingers making me shiver. "You're beautiful," he murmured, sliding my hair to the side and pressing a kiss to my nape.

I shivered again.

He took my hand, led me from the room and through the nearest exit into the moonlit night. "Where are we going?" I asked, the quiet of the evening settling all around us.

Leo didn't answer, just tugged me forward, and just when I was going to ask again, we moved behind a partition, and I felt my eyes sting again.

A table and chairs. More candles.

And a private view of . . . "Luna," I murmured.

He smiled, tucking my hair behind my ear, moving closer to slip his arm around my waist. "Yes," he said, "she's up there." A beat. "With babies."

And with that, he handed me a pair of night binoculars, and I focused on her nest.

Sure enough, there were babies there.

"Oh, my God," I whispered. "They're so cute. *Leo.*"

"*Jesse,*" he warned.

"I love you."

He took the binoculars from me and set them on the table. Then he took my hand and tugged me to him, placing my hand over his chest. "Feel that?" he asked roughly.

His heart thundered beneath my palm. "Yes," I whispered.

"It beats for you."

A tear slipped down my cheek, and he wiped it away.

"I love you," he said. "I toppled headfirst into it under the moonlight. It grew in the sunshine, winding through every nerve. I went from being half a person, from hardly living, to being half of *something*, of something incredible." He bent, catching more tears with his lips, his words breathed onto my skin. "I know that it's way too soon to be saying this, but know that one day, you'll be my wife. One day, you'll be mine in every way—"

"I am yours already," I said softly. "In every way."

His mouth was gentle as he kissed his way along my jaw. "I don't want you to think I would choose anyone else. Because you're so much more than I could have ever dreamed of."

My breathing hitched.

"Yes," I said.

He froze, leaned back enough to see my eyes. "Yes, what?"

"Yes, I'll marry you."

We'd wasted so much time. I wouldn't waste anymore. I was holding on to this man, onto my happiness, onto the life I deserved.

So, yes, I'd marry him.

Without hesitation.

He grinned, that special Leo smile, and said, "I was hoping you'd say that because—" He pulled out a ring.

Not a diamond band.

But plain black silicone with silver streaks. Something I could wear on every mission. Something I could have on me always.

He cleared his throat. "I could get you a diamond, something with bling and—"

I pressed a finger to his mouth.

"I don't want diamonds," I said. "I just want you."

"Thank God," he exclaimed, and then he tugged me flush against him, wrapped his big, strong arms around me, and we danced to the sounds of our heartbeats . . . and the tune of Luna's screech.

It was perfect.

It was fantasy.

It was reality.

EPILOGUE

PART TWO

Lily

"What are you doing?"

I glanced up at the open door to my office and knew my expression was guilty, but it was just so sweet! "Nothing," I said, wiping my eye and affecting casualness as Hannah moved toward me.

Slyly, I minimized the screen where I'd been—admittedly—spying on Leo and Jesse.

They were just so sweet.

Leo was so sweet.

I'd helped him with the dress and shoes, Hannah with filling Jesse's room with flameless candles and flowers.

He'd picked out the necklace, though he'd let me peek into the box.

I wasn't sure what the deal with owls was, but considering Jesse hadn't stopped touching it the entire time I'd spied on them as they'd walked across the courtyard, I knew she was happy with it.

Hannah rested a hip on my desk, her eyes flicking to my screen.

Ha.

Nothing to see here.

Her eyes flicked back to mine, something I couldn't read in her expression. Something that turned out to be sneaky. Because she asked, "You want to get some food?" and when I nodded and stood up, she reached for the mouse and opened the screen.

Which was on the camera feed of Leo and Jesse.

They'd been standing close together before, Jesse crying after what had probably been sweet words from Leo (damn cameras without audio, otherwise I could have listened in), but now they were dancing under the moonlight, their arms wrapped tightly around each other.

I sighed happily.

Seriously. So. Sweet.

Hannah glared down at me. "You're impossible."

"Because I have a heart and love a romantic ending?"

A roll of gorgeous hazel eyes, her blond ponytail fluttering behind her when she shook her head. "Come on," she said, clicking to close the camera feed rather than just minimizing it. "Let's eat."

I stuck out my bottom lip. "I don't want to."

Hannah sighed. "What *do* you want?"

You.

I was desperate to say it, but I knew that it wouldn't make the least bit of difference. Hannah didn't do relationships, and she certainly didn't do relationships with subordinates.

But I'd been in love with her from the moment I'd laid eyes on her.

See? I was a hopeless romantic.

I'd walked into KTS six years before, ready for my training, and had seen her knocking a man nearly twice her size to the mats in the gym. She hadn't struggled or breathed hard or even ended up with a hair out of place.

I'd arrested, felt my heart roll over and expose its vulnerable underbelly.

Then she'd smiled.

And I'd fallen deep.

She was smart, beautiful, funny, kind . . . and closed down to anything that resembled love. At least overtly, because I knew she loved our entire team. She would die to ensure that we would live, and do it in a heartbeat.

So, the love was there.

Just perhaps, not the romantic love.

And that was the love I was desperate for.

Unfortunately, I was beginning to think that wasn't going to happen. Grimacing, I grabbed my cell and started for the door.

Hannah sighed again. "What is it?"

I frowned, glanced back over my shoulder. "What's what?"

"Why are you doing Sad Face?"

I couldn't tell her, so I just said, "You interrupted my quota of romance for the day." I chuckled. "Of course, I have Sad Face."

Hannah strolled over to me, not stopping until she was close enough for me to see the faint scar just above her cheekbone. "Tell me the truth, Lily."

If only.

She narrowed her eyes.

I started to turn away, to hit that exit, and—

Then I was pinned to the wall, her hands on my shoulders, her body almost flush to mine. My heart skipped and began pounding rapidly. The backs of my knees went sweaty. The hair on my arms raised.

"Tell me." Her hazel eyes had darkened, more chocolate than the usual green.

I melted, felt her body move closer, pressing into mine, making my pussy clench and my skin tighten. "It's nothing," I managed to croak out.

"*Lily*," she warned, fingers gripping a little tighter.

My throat went tighter, and my answer was more rasp than that. "I think you know."

She growled. "Tell me."

And the truth just flew out of me. "I'm in love with you," I whispered.

Her eyes went wide; her mouth fell open.

But she didn't move, didn't say a word. At least not until I found myself lifting a hand, tracing my thumb lightly over that scar.

As though I could heal the old wound.

Heal *all* her old wounds.

She shuddered, her breath hot and damp on my lips . . . and then her mouth found mine.

—Scorching the Earth, December 28th, 2020

SCORCHING THE EARTH

Hannah and Lily's story is coming December 28th, 2021!

Preorder at www.books2read.com/ScorchingTheEarth

———

Hate missing Elise's new releases? Love contests, exclusive excerpts and giveaways?

Then signup for Elise's newsletter here!

http://eepurl.com/bdnmEj

———

KTS SERIES

Prequel Novella
Fire and Ice (Hurt Anthology)

Full Length Books
Riding The Edge
Crossing The Line
Leveling The Field
Scorching The Earth (December 28th, 2021)

ALSO BY ELISE FABER

Billionaire's Club **(all stand alone)**

Bad Night Stand

Bad Breakup

Bad Husband

Bad Hookup

Bad Divorce

Bad Fiancé

Bad Boyfriend

Bad Blind Date

Bad Wedding

Bad Engagement

Bad Bridesmaid

Bad Swipe (June 28th, 2021)

Gold Hockey **(all stand alone)**

Blocked

Backhand

Boarding

Benched

Breakaway

Breakout

Checked

Coasting

Centered

Charging

Caged

Crashed (July 27th, 2021)

Cycled (October 5th, 2021)

Breakers Hockey (all stand alone)

Broken

Boldly (August 31st, 2021)

KTS Series

Fire and Ice (Hurt Anthology, stand alone)

Riding The Edge

Crossing The Line

Leveling The Field

Love, Action, Camera (all stand alone)

Dotted Line

Action Shot

Close-Up

End Scene

Meet Cute

Love After Midnight (all stand alone)

Rum And Notes

Virgin Daiquiri

On The Rocks

Sex On The Seats

Life Sucks Series (all stand alone)

Train Wreck

Hot Mess

Dumpster Fire

Clusterf*@k (August 16th, 2021)

Roosevelt Ranch Series **(all stand alone, series complete)**

Disaster at Roosevelt Ranch

Heartbreak at Roosevelt Ranch

Collision at Roosevelt Ranch

Regret at Roosevelt Ranch

Desire at Roosevelt Ranch

Phoenix Series **(read in order)**

Phoenix Rising

Dark Phoenix

Phoenix Freed

Phoenix: LexTal Chronicles **(rereleasing soon, stand alone, Phoenix world)**

From Ashes

In Flames

To Smoke (October 18th, 2021)

Stand Alones

Someday, Maybe (YA)

ABOUT THE AUTHOR

USA Today bestselling author, Elise Faber, loves chocolate, Star Wars, Harry Potter, and hockey (the order depending on the day and how well her team -- the Sharks! -- are playing). She and her husband also play as much hockey as they can squeeze into their schedules, so much so that their typical date night is spent on the ice. Elise changes her hair color more often than some people change their socks, loves sparkly things, and is the mom to two exuberant boys. She lives in Northern California. Connect with her in her Facebook group, the Fabinators or find more information about her books at www.elisefaber.com.

facebook.com/elisefaberauthor

amazon.com/author/elisefaber

bookbub.com/profile/elise-faber

instagram.com/elisefaber

goodreads.com/elisefaber

pinterest.com/elisefaberwrite

www.ingramcontent.com/pod-product-compliance
Lightning Source LLC
Chambersburg PA
CBHW022140240626
47153CB00007B/2433